McKENDREE

McKENDREE

by Sandra Belton

Greenwillow Books

An Imprint of HarperCollins *Publishers*

For every song there is a melody;
for every book-to-be there is an editor.
Heaven smiled on me when Virginia Duncan Burton
said "Yes," to McKendree
and continued so skillfully to hum in my ear.

The excerpt from "My People" by Langston Hughes
on page 169 is from *Collected Poems* by Langston Hughes,
Copyright © 1994 by the Estate of Langston Hughes,
reprinted by permission of Alfred A. Knopf, a Division
of Random House, Inc.

McKendree

The text of this book was set in Waldbaum MT.

Library of Congress Cataloging-in-Publication Data
Belton, Sandra.
McKendree / by Sandra Belton.
p.   cm.
"Greenwillow Books."
Summary: In 1948, while spending the summer with her
aunt in West Virginia to find her family roots, Tilara Haynes finds new
beginnings and self-love in an unexpected place:
an old folks' home called McKendree.
ISBN 0-688-15950-8   1. Nursing homes—Fiction.
2. Self-esteem—Fiction. 3. Aunts—Fiction.
4. Afro-Americans—Fiction. 5. West Virginia—Fiction.
I. Title.   PZ7.B4197Mad   2000
[Fic]—dc21   99-24456   CIP

10 9 8 7 6 5 4 3 2 1
First Edition

In loving memory of my father,
Alphonso David Belton, M.D.

"McKendree."

It was the first word the little girl in the shadows of the tree had been able to make out. But the word made no sense. She took one step closer so she could hear more, being careful to stay close to the tree that hid her.

"Who's McKendree?" one of them said.

"Yeah. Wh-who's McKendree?"

"McKendree ain't a who. It's a place."

"Don't say 'ain't.' My nana says it's not a word and that people who say it are dummies."

"You're the dummy. You thought McKendree was a person."

The three children the girl watched and strained to hear lay just outside the shade of the big maple tree that hid her. Three five-year-old bodies like hers. Three summer-kissed bodies drawing their own shadows on the garden of grass that had been their afternoon place.

"How come you know McKendree's a place?" said the girl among the three. A girl with a bright yellow ribbon holding back curls that danced with every breeze.

1

"I know 'cause M'Dear told me," one of the boys answered. He was squinting so the others would know just by looking at him that what he said was true.

"What'd she tell you?"

"She told me McKendree is where Honeydipper Man lives now."

"Wh-who's that?" said the other boy. His words spilled out in soft little pieces. "Who's th-th-the Honeydipper Man?"

"He's the one who used to walk up and down the street singing all the time!" the knowing boy said. "Don't you know anything?" He looked at the other boy through his frown.

"Is that wh-why he lives at McK-K-Kendree?"

"No," said knowing boy, his voice bored with being the only one knowing things. "Honeydipper Man lives there 'cause he's old and ain't got no place else to live."

The small heads came closer together as the three thought about what it might be like to be old. Or to walk up and down the street singing and having no place to live.

The little face of the girl in the shadows pushed forward as far as it could to get a better look at the yellow-ribbon girl. The girl who was the same color as the china white

2

baby dolls. The ones the girl in the shadows found under her tree every Christmas morning. "Look at your beautiful baby doll," her father would say, patting the china white baby doll face with his big chocolate hand.

"Does everybody go to McKendree when they get old?" asked yellow ribbon.

"I don't know," knowing boy said. "Maybe."

For a while the rustle of birds returning to their maple tree home was the only sound.

"I'm not going to McKendree when I get old," yellow ribbon said, breaking the quiet.

"Me, neither," said knowing boy. He stood up, ready to move someplace new. "And you know what else? I'm never gonna get old, neither!"

"Me, neither," said yellow ribbon, getting up and brushing the grass from her red-and-yellow dress.

"Wh-wh-where y'all goin'?" asked soft words. His eyes followed every move yellow ribbon made. Just like the two eyes in the shadow of the tree.

"I'm gonna go catch me a butterfly," said knowing boy, running off into the stretch of grass. "That's what I'm gonna do."

"Me, too!" said yellow ribbon, taking off behind him.

"W-w-w-wait for me!" said soft words, hurrying to his feet.

The feet behind the tree itched to follow the others. But they didn't move. The little girl remained as she had been, still and silent in the cool afternoon shadows. She satisfied herself once more by only watching as the other three skipped and chased across the warm grass. Away from the shade umbrella of the maple tree. Away from all thoughts of McKendree.

SUMMER
1948

1

Tilara stared at her reflection, watching herself drift across the summer greens of the passing mountains.

A moving-picture star.

Thinking this, she saw her mouth bend into a small smile.

In the shadows of the window mirror of her little train room—a roomette, Papa had called it—Tilara studied the familiar details of herself: the dark chocolate face framed by tightly coiled strands of hair. The nut brown eyes. Haynes eyes. Eyes that had smiled from her father's face when he kissed her good-bye at the train station and that she would see in Aunt Cloelle, who would be waiting when the train ride was over.

Tilara turned from the window and leaned back against her seat. Closing her eyes, she took the picture of her reflected self into her thoughts and tried to imagine herself as Mr. Morris had called her when he brought her a breakfast tray that morning.

"My special service for every pretty young lady,"

he said, moving expertly in his starched white jacket to arrange food on the pulled-out-from-the-wall table.

Pretty young lady.

"Yessirree," Mr. Morris said. "I bet the boys back home are lined up outside your door!"

Tilara kept her eyes on the plate with the three kinds of bread on it.

"If there's anything else you want, just call me," Mr. Morris said, shutting the door to the little room as he left.

It was then that Tilara had started looking at herself in the window mirror. She watched herself spread jam on the muffin and lift it to her mouth. She saw the glass of juice fit against her lips, tilt forward, and slowly empty. Soon the picture-in-picture reflections of the window made it easier to imagine that she was what Mr. Morris had said: a pretty young lady.

But in her heart she knew better.

Tilara had grown up looking at reflections of someone she had been told was the loveliest woman who ever lived. A person whose pictures lined the wall along the stairs and almost filled the top of the piano in the living room. Someone whose portrait showed skin the color of cream, hair that hung to

8

her waist in silky brown curls, and wide eyes the color of gray smoke.

The pictures were of Tilara's mother. The woman Papa still talked to through the pictures.

"Don't you remember her eyes, Tee?" Papa would ask as he smiled at the person in the dining-room portrait. "Smoking pearls, I used to call them." He would chuckle. "You liked hearing that, didn't you, Lindy?" he would say to the portrait, seeming to forget that it was Tilara who was at the table with him and not Belinda Cross Haynes, his wife who had died when her daughter was not yet two years old.

Tilara couldn't remember anything about her mother, even though she had tried and tried. She had stood in front of the portrait many times, commanding it to bring a memory of her mother. But the picture only echoed the words she had heard her father say again and again: "Lindy was what you call a beautiful woman. A *truly* beautiful woman."

Her father's words and the everywhere pictures told Tilara that she could never be pretty. Being pretty was to look like the unplayed-with china white baby dolls that slept on the shelves of Tilara's closet. Images she saw as the opposite of herself.

Now, even in the graceful shadows of a reflection,

Tilara could see no other picture of herself but the one she always carried inside. It was her most powerful image. It wrapped around most of her joys, even the one of welcome she knew she would get at the end of her ride.

"Here's my Tilara," Aunt Cloelle would say. It was what she always said after their time apart. "My sweet Tilara. Just look at my baby!"

Tilara blew her breath onto the window. "Yeah," she muttered to the uneven puddle of fog settling on top of her reflection. "Just look at me."

She turned away from her window mirror. After a moment the muffled chant of the steel wheels racing down the tracks caught her up in a new rhythm.

So what, who cares. So what, who cares. So what, who cares. . . .

When Mr. Morris came to pick up her luggage, Tilara followed him into the narrow Pullman corridor.

"Do we have much farther to go?" she asked.

"Almost there," he called over his shoulder. "We just passed McKendree. Prince is right around the corner."

McKendree.

The word hummed in the back of her mind. Something both forgotten and remembered. And pushed back again as Mr. Morris kept on.

"Been quite awhile since you were in the middle of all of these grand West Virginia hills," he said. "Your aunt says you haven't been this way since you were little. No more than five, she said."

Tilara stared at Mr. Morris with wide eyes. How did he know she had an aunt? Or that she had been here before? How did he know anything about her?

Mick Morris placed Tilara's bags in line with the others stacked by the door and turned to her. His eyes twinkled at the surprise he saw in her face.

"Your aunt Cloelle and I have known each other for years," he said. He stretched out the *l*s in her aunt's name as if enjoying the sound of it.

Clo-llle.

"Aunt Clo ... um, she didn't tell me...." Tilara felt her words stumbling.

Mick Morris patted Tilara's shoulder. "Probably figured I'd tell you myself. That's what I meant to do right after you boarded, but I got so busy with everything. Then this morning when I brought in your breakfast—"

He knows Aunt Cloelle. That's why he served me breakfast in my room. She asked him to.

11

The thought crowded Tilara's mind and made her miss some of Mr. Morris's words.

"—your visit," he was saying.

"I'm sorry, Mr. Morris," she said. "What about my visit?"

"Cloelle sure is looking forward to it," he said. "Yessirree. That she is."

"I can hardly wait to get there," Tilara said, her words sure for the first time.

Mr. Morris undid the latches of the top half of the door and opened it. Summer breezes quickly filled the space.

"A fine summer is ahead," he said. "Yessirree, a fine summer."

Yessirree. A welcoming song. The word drew Tilara's eyes to the true smile on Mick Morris's handsome face.

"Yessirree," she whispered as she turned toward the sweet rushing air and felt her own smile become real.

Tilara smiled her thanks as she took the hand Mr. Morris extended and let him guide her onto the little metal stool he had placed between the last step of the Pullman car and the ground. Once on the platform, she looked eagerly across the scattered, welcoming faces. But it was the sound of their voices that grabbed her attention.

"She came in right on time today."

"There he is, over there! Hey, Sonny!"

"Y'all have a nice trip?"

"Sure feels good to be here."

She might have heard the same words at the train station back home. But never the rhythms. The slow, rolling beats and floating tones. Like a special mountain music under the perfect blue sky.

Then came the sound she had been waiting for. "Tilara! Tilara!"

Cloelle Haynes's voice rang across the platform as she rushed forward. Then she caught her niece in her arms. At once Tilara was filled with the smells of lilacs and jasmine. Smells of her childhood when Cloelle had lived with them in Boston to take care of her.

Holding Tilara by her shoulders, Cloelle stepped back to study her niece as if she were a picture in a frame. "My sweet Tilara. Just look at my baby!" Again she pulled her close.

In her aunt's safe embrace, Tilara remembered her thoughts and smiled.

Finally breaking away, Cloelle ran her fingers

along Tilara's cheeks. After a long moment she spoke almost as if to herself. "Tilara, my love, you're growing into such a beauty!"

Tilara looked into the face so much like her own. The same deep brown color, the same almond eyes. The same full lips now broken apart in a wide, welcoming grin. A face wrapped in so much love that she could not judge or deny. Without a word she hugged her aunt again and said, "Oh, Aunt Clo, it's like I've been waiting my whole life to be here."

Mr. Morris walked over to where the two stood together. Cloelle reached out to take his hand. "Mick, thank you for watching over my niece," she said. "It was a relief to know my baby was in your hands."

"My pleasure. You can't imagine how good it was to offer services to someone who didn't think my name was Porter!"

Tilara watched her aunt and Mr. Morris laughing together. She noticed the way his hand lingered on Cloelle's arm.

"Can we expect you on Sunday?" Cloelle asked.

"You can count on it," Mick Morris said. "Yessir-ree. I'd never pass up an opportunity to dine with two lovely women!" Turning to Tilara, he said, "It was delightful to have you aboard, and I'm going to look forward to getting to know you better."

Tilara could feel the grin settling on her face. "I'm looking forward to getting to know you, too."

Mr. Morris picked up his stepping stool and climbed on the train. His "Allllll aboard!" rang in the air.

"See you Sunday, ladies!" he called, waving with one hand and holding on to the inside railing of the Pullman car with the other as the train moved slowly down the track.

Cloelle gave her niece one more quick hug before leading the way to the baggage cart and then to her car for the final leg of the journey.

March

"Aw, com'on, Georgia. Don't be like that."

The girl turned away as the boy ran his finger down her cheek. His smile got bolder as he felt the soft smoothness.

"Like what?" the girl said. Her question teased, and a smile was in her voice.

The boy lowered his eyelids. It was a move he had practiced in front of his mirror without knowing until now how to use it. Then he ran his finger under her chin to make her face him again. "Like you have to turn away from me," he said. His voice teased back.

The girl stared into the half-opened honey-gold eyes. Her look for being in control. "I don't have to do nothing, March Jackson," she said.

He bent closer to her face. "But I do," he said.

She could feel his words as he pressed his lips against the corner of her mouth. She had time to breathe just one word before he covered her lips completely with his own: "March."

March and Georgia. Two friends who had grown up

together. Buddies with each other and the big maple tree under which they now stood. The sturdy trunk they leaned against had been home base for hard-won races. The thick umbrella of leaves that had been a favorite cooling-off spot now provided a private space away from nosy eyes.

It wasn't a first kiss for either of them. Both March and Georgia were popular in their crowd. The most sought-after prizes of spin-the-bottle explorations at birthday parties and in smelly cloakrooms. But it was a first shared kiss. A new discovery in their shared world.

Lost to everything but themselves, neither was aware of two others also standing together. These two stood at the kitchen window of the house at the other end of the yard, watching the figures in the lacy shadows of the old tree. The younger of the two was March's father, Jimmy Jackson. Sipping his third cup of coffee, he watched and remembered his own young times. And he worried.

Jimmy Jackson turned to his friend. "I'm beginning to think these kids have too much time on their hands," he said. "What do you think?"

The older man raised eyebrows becoming silver like his hair. "I think young love can be a wondrous thing," he said.

17

"Well, Dr. P.," Jimmy Jackson said, "seeing what they're doing in the bold light of day, I think we're going to have to help these kids find some other wondrous way to spend the long summer ahead."

After a long moment the two decided to honor the private moment on which they had intruded. They moved away from the window to finish their coffee somewhere else.

Realizing nothing but the newness of their feelings, the two under the tree kissed again.

2

"Oh, Aunt Clo, it's ... it's wonderful! I love it here."

Tilara stood at the edge of Cloelle's back porch, her eyes wide as she looked at the scene in front of her: curving mountains in the distance, their green thickness creating a ridge of blue. The grassy valley beneath, rolling with more shades of green than she had ever imagined. The now-and-then bursts of pink rhododendron shrubs. And the wildflowers scattered everywhere like purple and yellow butterflies frozen in time.

Cloelle smiled. "I call it my outrageous garden," she said.

"Outrageous?"

"Absolutely. It's outrageous for me to claim all this divine beauty as *my* garden," Cloelle said, "but I do. Every outrageously gorgeous inch of it. That's one reason I've never fenced in my little yard. I don't want it ever to be clear where my little plot of land ends and the other begins."

Still looking out, Tilara sat next to her aunt on the porch steps. "How'd you find it?" she asked.

19

Cloelle looked at Tilara through a frown. "Don't you know what this place is?"

"It's . . . it's your house, isn't it?"

"Kenneth never told you about this place?" Cloelle looked out into the meadow and shook her head. "That brother of mine is really something." She sighed.

Cloelle stretched out her legs and rested back on her elbows. "Mama grew up here, Tee," she said. "Your grandmother. She was born in this house and probably played out there in that lovely outrageous garden."

"Did you and Papa grow up here, too?"

"Mama moved after she got married. Your father and I grew up in Warren Springs."

"Papa *did* tell me that," Tilara said, smiling at Cloelle.

"I'm glad to hear Kenneth hasn't forgotten everything about his roots," Cloelle said, pretending to be relieved.

"The last time we came here you lived in Warren Springs."

Cloelle's eyebrows raised. "You remember the house in Warren Springs?" she asked, looking at Tilara. "You were only five when you and your father drove down that summer."

Tilara rested back on her elbows. "I sort of remember," she said. "I mean, it's not all that clear, but I do remember that you lived in a town. Not here. I would never forget being here. And Papa *does* talk about Warren Springs sometimes."

Tilara stretched out her legs, lining them up beside Cloelle's. "Does it get lonesome being so far away from everything?"

Cloelle stroked Tilara's arm. "It's not as isolated as it might look. There're several houses in this valley." She looked out into the horizon. "We're tucked in here together, yet still by ourselves. That's one of the things I love about living here. Another thing is being close to both of my jobs."

"Jobs?" Tilara knew her aunt taught business courses in a high school; she didn't know of any other job she had.

"Besides teaching, I work in the office at Mc-Kendree."

McKendree.

The word tugged at Tilara's memory for a second time.

"The old folks' home. I work there several days a week doing business-type things, like keeping the books."

"But not in the summer, right?"

21

Cloelle heard the anxiety in Tilara's voice. "Only a few hours each week. Not nearly enough to notice."

Tilara picked at a thread on the shorts she had changed into after she unpacked.

"McKendree won't cramp our style one bit, Tee." Cloelle got up and then reached for Tilara's hand to pull her up. "Promise."

Tilara smiled and flicked the thread to the wind.

Cloelle stretched. "Feel like picking some cherries?" she asked.

"Sure," Tilara said, getting ready to follow her aunt into the yard.

"Grab one of those baskets." Cloelle pointed to the uneven stack of for-summer baskets piled near the kitchen door.

The grass was a soft, warm cushion under Tilara's bare feet as they walked to a tree near the edge of Cloelle's neatly mowed yard. The tree was fat with plump black cherries.

"When I was little," Cloelle said, picking from a branch almost touching the top of her head, "and we came to visit Granny—your *great*-grandmother—we picked cherries from this same tree."

22

Tilara nibbled on the handful of cherries she pulled from branches brushing her shoulder. "I bet Papa never picked cherries," she said. "I can't imagine him doing anything with food but eating it!"

"You mean my brother is still too pitiful to do anything in the kitchen but dirty up dishes?" Cloelle shook her head and chuckled. "I shouldn't be surprised. Mama never made him do anything around the house. She spoiled him the same way she spoiled our father."

Tilara rolled cherry seeds around in her mouth. "What was Papa like when he was a kid?" she asked.

"Pretty much like he is now: hardworking, stuffy, and trying to run everybody's life," Cloelle said, laughing at her own description.

Tilara's giggle was bubbled breaths of surprise. She had never heard her father spoken of in that way.

"Papa *is* stuffy," she said, taking strength from her aunt's words. "He doesn't even loosen his tie while he sits in the parlor at night just reading or working on his sermons or something like that."

"Yep, that's my brother," Cloelle said, chuckling again. "And you might as well admit he's controlling, too, because everybody who knows him knows that he is."

Cloelle saw the shadow of frustration pass across Tilara's face as she continued. "I used to think being that way had something to do with Kenneth's being a minister," she said. "But then I remembered he had *always* been that way. Even when we were kids."

She moved closer to Tilara to pick from the cluster of cherries Tilara had reached into. "It's not how he means to be. Most of the time I don't think he even realizes what he's doing. It's just the way he is."

"Yeah," Tilara said quietly, plucking the cherries with a greater force.

Just the way he is.

Tilara pictured her father as he was every Sunday morning: standing in the pulpit with his robed, outstretched arms welcoming "sinners to come and join the fold," his deep voice booming across the entire space of the Boston church where he had been the pastor for almost twenty years. The same voice that boomed throughout their house every day, calling out, reminding, suggesting, or complaining.

Controlling.

Tilara knew better than anyone how the Reverend Dr. Kenneth Haynes took charge of almost everybody and everything in his life. His church, the big house—the parsonage, he called it—where they lived, and his daughter. He set the rules for Miss Katy, the housekeeper who had cleaned and cooked for them for as long as Tilara could remember and who kept everything exactly as Pastor Haynes wanted it. He decided how the furniture should be arranged and where his carefully tended potted plants should be placed. He planned the menus and made out the grocery lists. He even decided how the parsonage telephone should be answered. "Always let them know whom they've reached," he would call out if Tilara picked up the receiver and simply said "Hello" and not "Reverend Haynes's residence."

Controlling.

Her father's controlling filled her closet with a neat line of brown and navy blue skirts. It set hours for her to spend time reading even after all her homework was finished. It kept Tilara from cutting her hair to have the bangs she wanted so much. "You don't have the right kind of hair for bangs," he informed Tilara. Kenneth Haynes's fatherly controlling covered everything.

Just the way he is.

Now, for the first time ever, Tilara was going to be spending time away from her father. A whole summer's worth of time. Past summers had brought Cloelle north to Boston for the family visits. But the last time she had come—it had been two summers ago—Cloelle had started persuading her brother to let Tilara come south. "Tilara needs an opportunity to get in touch with the family roots, Kenny," Cloelle had said again and again, calling Tilara's father by a name so out of character Tilara wanted to giggle every time she heard it.

But she didn't giggle. Every time she heard her father and aunt discussing The Visit, she prayed. A silent prayer deep from her heart, begging that she would be allowed to go. When her father finally agreed, Tilara had almost shouted with joy.

But the Reverend Dr. Kenneth Cullen Haynes didn't tolerate shouting in his house. Only in his church.

"Tilara, your basket overfloweth!"

Cloelle's words, so much like ones her brother used in his pulpit, pulled Tilara back to the moment. She looked beyond her marooned-tipped fingers to see mounds of fruit around her feet.

"Sorry, Aunt Clo," she said, bending to pick up the cherries that had spilled onto the ground. "I guess I was thinking more than watching."

"No harm done," Cloelle said, helping to gather

the fruit. "They'll all be the same, bubbling together in that cobbler, but we do need another basket."

As Tilara carried her packed basket to the porch, she could feel her aunt's eyes on her. Just as she could always feel Miss Katy's eyes on her whenever she stopped in the kitchen after school to get a snack from the refrigerator. But she knew the watching eyes near the cherry tree were different.

Aunt Clo wouldn't care at all if I rummaged through her refrigerator.

"Get a big basket, baby," Cloelle called. "We want to make sure we have enough cherries."

"This is going to be a fat cobbler," Tilara called back, looking through the pile of differently shaped wicker containers. "I hope we can eat it all."

"We won't have to," Cloelle said. "My friend Bessie said she and her daughter Sylvie might drop by later. Sylvie's about your age; she'll be starting high school in the fall. And any other leftovers will be devoured by Mick when he joins us for Sunday dinner."

Tilara remembered the way Mr. Morris and Aunt Cloelle had looked at each other at the train station. How his fingers had rested on her aunt's arm. The picture carried her smile into her voice.

"Aunt Cloelle, will this be enough cherries to bake a cobbler big enough for Mr. Mawrrrris?" she called, trying out a drawl as she held up the basket she had selected.

"I think so," Cloelle answered, her smile bright and carrying its own message.

Basket in hand, Tilara stood for a moment at the top of the steps leading to the yard. Closing her eyes, she breathed in the mountain air with its scents of ripe cherries, summer wildflowers, and meadow grass. Smells of the outrageous garden.

And I'll be here the entire summer. Every beautiful, outrageous summer day.

Suddenly Tilara wanted to jump from the porch into the yard. She hesitated, seeing her father's hand in front of her, holding her back and reminding softly, "Young ladies don't bound, Tilara. They descend stairs gracefully."

Tilara was still for a moment. Then, slowly and carefully, she walked down the porch steps into the green, welcoming softness below.

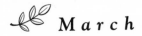 # March

March faced his father, trying to focus on what he had heard. Something about going with Dr. P. to McKendree? A few days every week this summer?

No. That couldn't have been what his father had said. That made no sense. None at all.

He kept standing there, looking at his father. Waiting for him to speak again. To make sense.

Jimmy Jackson smiled at his son. "It'll be a good opportunity for you to get involved with something worthwhile, March," he said. "A good change of pace, going to McKendree. And only a few days a week."

A few days every week? You must be crazy! I don't want to go to McKendree ever. Never.

The words raced through March's head as he clenched his teeth behind lips held tight.

His father went on. "There's a lot of good you can do there. As a young person, just being around will help a great deal. Make the old folks feel better. And by talking to them . . ."

The anger kept growing. March could feel it crawling over him. It began to form into a ball, wanting to hurl itself forward. Finally March could no longer hold it back.

"How is that gonna be worthwhile?" He almost spit out the words. "Spending a summer in a dead place like Mc-Kendree—how's that gonna help anything? Hanging around a bunch of old people doesn't make any sense at all! It just stinks!"

His father's voice cracked across the space between them. "March! Don't forget who you're talking to," he said. He rested his gaze firmly on March's face, realizing for the first time that he hardly had to bend his head to look directly into his son's eyes.

The becoming man and his father stood without speaking. In the silence March decided on another approach. "Dad, it's just that I been thinking about all the stuff I could do around here this summer, you know . . ."

The new approach failed. Along with all the other clever, gentler pleading and promises. In the end it was for March just as it had started.

McKendree.

3

The soft knock on the screen door came just as Cloelle dug into the flaky covering of the steaming berries. "Bessie, your timing is perfect," she called out. "Com'on in. The door's open."

The woman and girl who walked in were reflections of each other: matching lilac-flowered dresses, white slipper shoes, and friendly eyes shining in plain, round faces.

Cloelle hugged the woman. "Bessie, did you smell my cobbler all the way in your kitchen?"

Bessie's wide grin revealed front teeth edged in gold. "Smelled like something 'bout ready to burn," she teased back. "I rushed on over here to see what I could do to save it."

A lively warmth followed the two through the door. Tilara smiled easily to the girl as the two women greeted each other. The girl smiled back.

Cloelle placed her hands on Tilara's shoulders. "Bessie, this is my niece," she said. "My Tilara."

Bessie extended both hands to Tilara. "Don't you think I know that?" she said, including Tilara in the warmth of her smile. "I would know that just meeting this pretty on the street. She looks like you, Clo, only better."

Tilara made herself look into the friendly face. "Hi, Miss Bessie," she said.

"Just Bessie, baby," the woman said, pulling Tilara close for a hug. "Cloelle and me, we're family. That makes you family, too."

Cloelle drew the girl into the circle. "And this is Sylvie," she said, "who never gets a chance to say much when her mama's around because her mama won't stop talking."

The girl's smile widened as her mother's had. "Hi," she said, looking at Tilara.

"My baby girl don't say much," Bessie said, gently rubbing her daughter's back, "only she's not really my baby. She's my next-to-oldest child and my oldest girl. Besides that, Sylvie is practically my right hand. I know she needs to get around young people more, and I'm always telling her to, but she seems to like sticking around the house and helping out. If all of my children were like her—"

"Maaa-ma . . ." Sylvie's words sang a plea to her mother as her face flushed with embarrassment.

Cloelle winked at Tilara. "See what I mean? It's impossible for Sylvie to get a word in with her mother around. Why don't the two of you go out on the front porch so you can have a real conversation while I show 'just Bessie' here what a real cobbler is supposed to taste like."

Tilara looked questioningly at Sylvie, who shrugged her agreement with the suggestion.

"Okay," Tilara said, "but make sure to save us some cobbler."

The happy ring in her voice made Cloelle smile as she dug once more into the golden crust.

The two girls looked out into the night. "Want to go for a walk?" Tilara asked, thinking this would at least give them something to do if talking turned out to be a problem.

"Okay," Sylvie said with another shrug.

They headed down the stone-and-dirt path that ran along the front of Cloelle's house. The smells and sounds of the summer night filled in the silence and made them comfortable.

"You got a pretty name."

Tilara grinned in the darkness, enjoying the southern rhythm of Sylvie's slow, floating words. "You like it? Um, I mean, thanks. I always thought my name was . . . well, just different. I never thought about it being pretty or anything."

She batted at a pair of dancing lightning bugs. "Sylvie is a pretty name, too."

"I like it a whole lot more than I like my middle name."

"What's your middle name?"

"Ozell," Sylvie said with a half moan. "I'm sure glad Mama and Daddy didn't make that my first name 'cause if they had, I wouldn't answer to nooo-body!"

Sylvie's "no" hung in the air, making both girls laugh.

"I promise I won't ever call you anything but Sylvie," Tilara said.

"And I won't call you nothing but Tilara," Sylvie said, "unless you like your middle name better."

"I don't have one, so Tilara will be just fine." Tilara fought the urge to float the sound of her name as Sylvie did. "Unless you want to call me Tee like Aunt Clo does."

"You like that better?" Sylvie said, her voice doubting it.

"I don't mind it." Tilara giggled. "Not like I would if my name were *Pi*-lara."

For a second there was nothing. Then the giggles of both girls floated above the gentle night sounds.

Hearing it, Tilara was reminded of Lena, her best friend, and a door to talking swung open wide.

About best friends.

"I know you'd like Lena—she's so much fun. And thinks of the craziest things to do! Like the time she got a whole bunch of us at school to stick our knives and forks under the lunchroom tables after we finished eating. We started doing it all the time. After a few days the teachers started going crazy. They even started checking kids leaving the cafeteria."

About places.

"It's okay to live in a city, I guess, and yeah, there's always stuff to do. But it's so special here— all these mountains and space. It's like ... like you're free."

About home ...

"Yeah, our house is right next door to Papa's church. Most of the time I don't mind it—I even forget being there. But stuff like playing records makes me remember. I have to turn the volume down so low I might as well not be playing them at all. Papa would have a fit if the music disturbed anything going on over at the church."

... and being away from home.

"Aunt Clo and I played some of her Nat King Cole records before dinner. Don't you just love him?

She let me turn up her Victrola as loud as I wanted. It's a wonder you didn't hear it over at your house!"

Their walk into the meadow and back again filled up with laughing, talking. Sharing. By the time they got back to the porch, neither of them felt ready to stop. They sat side by side on the steps.

"You ever been fishing?" Sylvie asked.

The thought of small creatures dangling on a hook at the end of a thin line made Tilara shudder. "Not ever," she said, hoping her feelings didn't show in her voice.

"I go all the time," Sylvie said. "There's a real good place near my house. Want to go sometimes?"

I really like Sylvie. She'll be fun to be with this summer. Maybe she won't notice if I ignore the fish.

Tilara swallowed. "Yeah. Maybe one day when, ah, when I'm not going to McKendree."

"McKendree? The old folks' home?" Sylvie wrinkled up her nose. "Y'all got kin over there?"

"No. Aunt Clo works over there some days, and I'll be going with her." Tilara began rubbing her arms against the chilling air. "Is it awful over there?"

Sylvie shrugged. "I don't know, but Mama prob'ly does. She used to go over there to see Miss Letty, a lady who went to our church. Miss Letty was in church every Sunday until she got so she couldn't get there on her own. She didn't have no family or nothing and nobody to help take care of her. I guess that's how come she ended up at Mc-Kendree."

Tilara wrapped herself tighter with her arms. "I'm not particular about going, but Aunt Clo has to, and since I'll be with her . . ." She looked at Sylvie. "It can't be all that bad. Folks live there."

"I guess . . ." Sylvie said, and shrugged. "Well, anytime you want to go fishing, let me know."

"I will," Tilara said. Shivering, she got up from the steps. "I'm ready for some cobbler. Want to go inside?"

Sylvie got up and brushed at the back of her dress. "Okay, Tilara," she said.

"Okay, Sylvie," Tilara said, stretching out the name to float a word of her own into the quieting night.

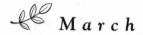 # March

He had failed. Nothing March had said or done had changed his father's mind about McKendree. He had really failed.

March Jackson knew very little about failure. Success was what he had had more of in his life than anything else. Success born from being the boy all the girls wanted to sit next to and all the boys wanted on their teams. March wasn't the fastest runner, strongest hitter, or greatest catcher. He wasn't the best anything. But he was always the most wanted. Teachers smiled when they called on March. They minded it less if he was the one caught cutting up in the back of the room.

Success followed March everywhere, especially to the mirror. "You sure named him right," Aunt Delilah had said to March's mother. "This boy is the spittin' image of Granddaddy March Jackson, and he was the best-looking man that's ever been in this family!" Success gave March his ready smile and easy way of speaking. It made him confident that in time he could bring everything he wanted his way.

Never failure. Never.

Now, standing in front of Morton's and seeing his reflection in the crowded display window, March remembered how things were supposed to be. The anger that had been walking with him as he went to meet his friends turned itself around, and a plan began to fill his thoughts.

Braxton. I can convince him to go. Knowing my man Braxton, he might even cook up a reason to like spending time with those dried-up old . . .

March smiled as his plan took shape.

Thumb'll go. He's too afraid of missing out on something not to go. Good old Thumb's always good for a laugh. And if he goes, Olivia will want to, too.

The smile became a grin.

And Georgia . . . sweet Georgia not so brown . . .

March used the open flap of his shirt to fan himself. To dry the sweat caused by the heat of his anger, now fading.

Georgia's after me. She'll go anywhere I'm going.

March checked himself again in the window mirror of Morton's. He wanted to look just right when he went inside to tell his friends about his great idea.

"Just once or twice a week," he said, speaking out loud to see how it would sound. "We all need to do something worthwhile. Anyhow, we have a whole summer to have fun."

Success twinkled in March's eyes as he reached out for the handle of the heavy glass door.

Success. As it always had, it made March free.

4

As their car eased along the winding two-lane road, Tilara watched the growing thickness of sugar maples, oaks, and white pines. "We're getting farther and farther away from everything," she said. "Why did they build the home for old folks so far away? Shouldn't it be nearer to town so it would be easy for people to visit?"

Cloelle sighed. "For one thing, this was the land the state designated for the colored old folks' home. The land set aside for the home for white folks is nearer town."

Tilara turned away from the window and rested back in her seat. "Papa hates that word," she said.

"What? Colored?"

"Umhmm. He doesn't particularly like 'Negro,' either. He says we should call ourselves 'black' like Dr. Du Bois does."

"Do you have a preference?" Cloelle asked, her eyes fastened on the road.

A memory flashed in Tilara's mind. The Baptist Assembly of her father's church. The gathering of all the deacons and trustees and their families. The photographer with his wobbly tripod and loud, commanding voice.

"All you men stand there in the back. That's right. Make a nice straight line behind the chairs. My, my, my. What a handsome group of Negro men we have here."

He pointed the women to the single row of chairs. "Now you ladies take your seats. Cross your right ankle over your left one so everybody'll be uniform. That's right. Oh, you're beautiful! Gentlemen, have you ever seen a finer-looking group of colored ladies?"

He directed the children to sit in a row on the floor in front of the women. Pointing to Tilara, who had seated herself at one end, he asked her to change positions. "Move next to the little girl in the green dress. That's right, the one in the middle. We don't want any of our pretty little black faces to get lost in the shadows."

Pictures of the Baptist Assembly were taken every year. The photos lined the top of the mantel in the parlor of the parsonage. Tilara hated them all.

"So, which do you prefer?" Cloelle's repeated question burst through the unwanted memory.

Tilara shrugged and mumbled, "I guess I prefer Tilara." Then she turned her head again to the window.

Tilara did not see her aunt's smile that followed. How it spread like warm honey across the face whose deep, rich hues matched her own.

Cloelle tightened her grip on the steering wheel. The remaining curves on the road to McKendree were tricky; a firm grip would be needed to maneuver them safely.

A ragged wooden fence marked the end of the road and beginning of the place. Cloelle parked next to the uneven gravel path, and they both got out. For a long moment Tilara stood beside the car without moving or speaking.

McKendree. The place for old folks. A place that had been carved from the woods that still bordered three of its sides. A lone, long, red-brick building tucked in the shadows of the West Virginia hills.

Beyond its sloping green lawn the building faced the New River, judged by many to be the oldest river in North America. It was known as the best fishing river in the county. Early-morning fishermen claimed that New River fish crowded the surface of the water doing a catch-me dance. But the river was calm and easy as it flowed by McKendree. Quiet like the land and the place.

"It's my belief that beauty is McKendree's special surprise," Cloelle said, enjoying the expression on Tilara's face.

"It is beautiful," Tilara said, her voice almost a whisper. "Not at all what I expected."

Cloelle gathered her papers from the backseat of the car. "Yes," she said, "there is something about this place . . . but unfortunately, much of it is what one might expect." With her free hand she reached for one of Tilara's. "Come. Take a look around so you can decide for yourself."

The "something" about McKendree stuck in Tilara's mind as she looked around.

What is it about this place?

McKendree was peaceful. Tilara knew this as soon as she stepped out of her aunt's car and heard the low hum of the river. She felt it in the river breezes that cooled her arms while she walked the length of the long porch. It warmed her inside when the frail woman sitting alone reached her hand out to Tilara and said, "Hi, darlin'. I'm so happy to see you."

There was also the quiet. When there was talking, it was soft. Slow. Movement from one place to another was the same way. Soft shoes padding across smooth floors. Slowly. Even the McKendree smells were quiet. No strong scents or spicy flavors hung in the air.

As she walked along a quiet corridor in the building, Tilara felt the loneliness and sadness of the place. She saw it in the face of the man who silently nodded his greeting when she walked past. His eyes had the look of someone lost—not the lost of wondering where he was; the lost of having no place to go or be.

Back in the privacy of her aunt's office, Tilara remembered Sylvie's Miss Letty and wanted to know more about the why of McKendree. "Are all the people here alone? I mean, have the rest of their families . . . um, died?"

"Some of the folks never had much family to begin with," Cloelle explained, "or lost track of them for one reason or another. And yes, others have lost all the family they did have."

Tilara studied her aunt's face as she listened.

"Then, too, baby, you have to remember that some of these people were born either in or shortly after the time of slavery. Tracking family was next to impossible in those times. For most of their years they had all they could do to survive, to support themselves. Many never owned property or had opportunities to accumulate much money. And when they got too old to make it on their own, well ..."

"They ended up here," Tilara finished.

"That's the size of it," Cloelle said, nodding.

Tilara watched her aunt settling in an office crowded with stacks of folders and ledger books and then gazed at the stretch of green beyond the long window.

"Mind if I wait for you down by the river?" she asked.

"I'll look for you there when I finish," Cloelle said. "I won't be too much longer."

As she walked beside the New River, Tilara thought about McKendree—what it was and what it wasn't. It was a pretty place even in its quiet loneliness and sadness. And it was peaceful. She could come there and be relaxed on the days her aunt had to be there.

McKendree wasn't Boston with its park festivals and beaches. But it wasn't Boston with its hot summer streets and manufactured list of things to do, either. Things dreamed up by the Reverend Kenneth Haynes, who endlessly warned Tilara that an idle mind was evil's workshop.

Yes, there really is something about McKendree. It's miles and miles away from Papa.

Smiling with her thoughts, Tilara sat on a thick patch of grass and took off her shoes. She rested back on her elbows, lifted her chin toward the sun, and closed her eyes. It was then that she felt a shadow cross her face and heard a voice. Startled, she looked up and said, "Excuse me?"

She found herself looking into a pair of eyes the color of honey. Eyes like none she had ever seen before.

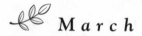 **M a r c h**

For most of the ride to McKendree, March was quiet. Having convinced his friends to join him in doing "something worthwhile," there was no need to keep up a front of being excited. He half listened to Braxton's stream of questions about McKendree and didn't care at all about Dr. P.'s answers; he hardly heard Thumb's usual jokes.

What he did do was think about his next move: how to get out of having to make this trip ever again.

Georgia guessed what was on his mind. She knew March too well to believe for a moment that he was voluntarily spending time at an old folks' home. She whispered this to him as they rode. March lowered his eyelids and boasted that he didn't do anything he didn't want to do. So she said nothing else and kept her doubts to herself.

Then, finally, they were there.

The unexpected loveliness of McKendree disarmed each of them. March was the first to recover, deciding not to join the others on a walk to look around. "Y'all go on," he said. "I'll catch up in a few minutes."

Shoving his hands in his pockets, he turned in the direction of the river. He made his way down the slope slowly, kicking at the grass as he walked.

The day was clear, the sky cloudless. A brilliant sun danced across the quiet river, dropping tiny jewels on the surface with each step. March took it all in as he walked. He spit on the ground and said his thoughts out loud. "Too bad all of this is wasted on old people."

Thoughts of his grandmother filled his mind. M'Dear. His perfect grandmother, who had lived next door until he was ten years old. Then, needing help, she had moved in with March and the rest of the family to be taken care of by her daughter, Marilyn, his mother.

He had watched his beloved M'Dear change from a woman who had baked the world's best oatmeal raisin cookies to a person who sometimes couldn't remember her last name. A person who had grown more like a child each day and who finally passed from this life without recognizing the daughter who held her hand through the last second.

"What a waste!" March said aloud again, kicking this time at the pain that twisted around his heart whenever he thought about M'Dear. Pain that made him hate any thought of being old.

"Excuse me?"

March lifted his head. He had been so deep in his thoughts he hadn't realized anyone was there. But someone was.

It was a girl. She was stretched out on the bank at the edge of the river. Her ebony silhouette against the blue-yellow sky at once filled his imagination. She was the loveliest girl he had ever seen.

5

Tilara scrambled to her feet. She pushed at her dress and took tiny steps backward, away from the boy standing so close he was almost touching her. Why had he come up on her like that, like he owned the place? Had he been talking to her? And why was he staring at her like that?

Tilara looked down, not wanting to stare back. She frowned at the grass, which no longer felt like a soft cushion but a prickly sheet, scratching at her toes. She fought the urge to rub her feet and pushed again at her dress instead.

The boy had made everything different. Who was he? Why he did just keep standing there, not saying anything?

The questions filled her mouth and made her look back into his face. But still she didn't speak. What did she want to say to this stranger with skin and eyes the color of honey?

Seeing her eyes directly across from his, March lost the words he had been ready to say, the "Hey, there, I'm March, and who are you?" that was supposed to come out of his mouth as easily as air. Trying to get them back, he cleared his throat.

"Excuse me?" Tilara said. The leftover question rushed out of her mouth.

Hearing her speak, March struggled again. He couldn't find words to finish even his thoughts. And he couldn't stop staring.

Tilara wanted to leave. To get back to the building and the safety of her aunt's office. Away from this boy who wouldn't stop gawking at her. What was wrong with him? With her?

She searched the ground with her eyes to see where she had tossed her shoes and saw them to one side of the boy. She reached forward. "Excuse me," she said again. "I need to get my shoes."

March stared at the hair that fell forward when she bent down beside him. Hair that was a cloud of brown. That's what he wanted to tell her: "Your hair is like a beautiful brown cloud." But clouds weren't brown. She would think he was crazy. He remained quiet and kept watching as she picked up the sandals near his foot and hooked them over her fingers.

Now that she had her shoes and could leave, Tilara decided she should be the one to say something. "I've got to go. Aunt Cloelle . . . she's probably waiting for me." It wasn't true, but it was all she could think of. She turned to make her way back up the slope.

Seeing her about to go away, March found words at last. "Wait," he said. "Aunt Cloelle—who's she?" It wasn't what he needed to know, but it was a beginning.

Tilara stopped, almost afraid to look into those staring eyes again. "She's my aunt," she said, turning only halfway. "She works here sometimes." Her words were little more than mumbles.

March watched as her long lashes rose and fell, and her fingers brushed pollen away from her cheek. He grew bolder, knowing he *had* to make her stay. "I came with somebody who works here, too," he said. "We all did. We just got out of Dr. P.'s car, and I was looking around—"

She hadn't intended to say anything, only to listen for as long as she had to, and then leave. But the name didn't fit McKendree. "Dr. P.?" she asked, turning to look into his face.

"Oh, his real name is Courtland. Dr. Adolphus Courtland." Now that they had started, March's words spilled out. "Of course, since neither of those names begins with a *P*, you probably think calling him Dr. P. is kind of strange."

March was getting lost in the gaze of her wide

brown eyes. He decided to watch the bee that was circling his hand.

"You see," he went on, his eyes on the bee, "when Dr. P.—only everyone probably called him Adolphus then because that's his name—when he was in medical school, he was the smartest guy in his class but real busy most of the time 'cause he was working his way through school. He said his class-mates always wanted his help, you know, like asking him to study with them, but he usually had to tell them he was too busy, you know, going to work and getting his own studying done."

Even to his own ears he was beginning to sound idiotic. But March found himself helpless to control the flow of words. Besides, they were working. She was still there.

"So they started teasin' him, you know, calling him a real pain, saying he was hurting them by not helpin' them study. They started callin' him Dr. Pain."

March watched the bee fly on. He imagined that he had sounded like an idiot even to the bee and that was why it left. But still he babbled on.

"When his children were little, he told them this story, they started callin' him Dr. P., and then every-body sort of . . ."

His words ran out. March took a deep breath and looked into her face. He smiled.

Tilara smiled back.

The sight of her smile. It brought him back. March was March. "I bet you're glad you asked," he said, his confidence again in place.

A small frown touched Tilara's nose and widened her nostrils.

"You know," he said, reading her face, "about Dr. P." The bottom in his voice that had almost disappeared earlier had returned.

"Oh," she said. "Yes. That was a . . . an interesting story."

For a moment Tilara could not stop herself from staring. Then she tore her eyes away from the dancing eyes and bright, confident smile. She no longer saw the honey-colored boy with the long story. Instead it was the face of Leland Persinger looking back at her.

Leland Persinger. The most wanted-for-a-boyfriend boy in all of eighth grade, just as he had been in seventh and sixth. And fifth. The memory of him whisked Tilara back in time.

It had been one day after school that fifth-grade year. Tilara, her best friend, Lena, and Pearl were walking arm in arm toward Dorchester Street, taking up all the space on the sidewalk.

"Here come Leland and Bobby," Pearl said, whispering as she always did whenever boys were the subject. Especially Leland. "Don't let them by."

Pearl was in the middle, with Lena on her right. Tilara was on the left, next to the edge of the sidewalk. She tried to pull her arm free, but Pearl held tight. "No, girl," she whispered. "Make them walk out in the street to get around us."

When it became clear that their path was blocked, the boys stopped. They were only breaths away from the girls' faces.

Bobby made a face and said, "Your arms stuck or something? Or do we have to move you out the way?"

Leland Persinger smiled. A twinkling-eyes smile, filled with the confidence of being the most wanted and knowing it. "Come on, Bobby," he said, stepping around Tilara into the gutter and pulling Bobby with him.

"Them silly girls make me sick," Bobby said as they walked around. "If it hadda been me by myself, I woulda moved them good."

Leland had laughed. "How come?" he said in his smooth-as-cream voice. "Lena's too skinny to push, Pearl's too ugly, and Tilara is too black."

Tilara is too black . . . too black . . . too black. . . .

As she remembered this, Tilara's eyes narrowed. She saw the smiling, honey-colored, knowing boy in front of her and realized more than ever that she had to get away.

"I have to go now," she said, turning in the direction of the building.

"Wait!" March stepped toward her. "I don't even know your name. What is it?"

"Tilara," she said without turning around.

"Tee-*lahra*," March repeated. His saying it made the name part of a melody.

The sound slowed her steps, outlining her folded shoulders and slightly bent head against the sky. For March the sight was a telling picture.

"That's it!" he said softly. An image of his cousin Cynthia passed through his mind. The cousin so shy she hardly spoke above a whisper, never really wanting to be heard. Seeing Tilara there on the slope, March was reminded of Cynthia as she often looked, standing at the edge of the family group with her bent-in shoulders and bent-down head, trying her best to fade from sight.

"Tilara's shy," he said again to himself. "Yeah, that's it." Sure in his discovery, he called to her. "Tilara, my name's March. March Jackson."

Tilara paused briefly and looked back over her shoulder. "Hi . . . um, I mean, it was nice to meet you," she said, and started walking again.

Watching, March said her name again, this time only for himself. The lovely, pleasing sound of it made him laugh out loud.

Tilara heard his laugh and felt his eyes on her as she hurried away. She never once looked back.

6

When Tilara reached the porch steps, she found her aunt waiting. She pretended not to see Cloelle's sly smile when she purred, "Looks like you might have had an interesting stroll by the river."

Tilara shrugged her shoulders and said nothing.

"You were talking to the young man, weren't you?" Cloelle said, persisting.

So? What if I was?

Tilara kept her sharp words inside and simply shrugged again, busying herself with the buckles on her sandals.

"Did you get a chance to introduce yourselves to each other?" Cloelle said, ignoring Tilara's message of silence.

"His name is March," Tilara said, her voice flat. "I don't remember what he said his last name was."

"Jackson," Cloelle said. "It's March Jackson."

Tilara looked at her aunt, wanting to ask, "Since you knew who it was, why were you asking me?" But her frown was the only reaction.

Cloelle saw the puzzled irritation on Tilara's face.

"I just wondered if the two of you had met," she said. "I knew March was one of the kids who came to McKendree today, and I thought I recognized him when I saw the two of you."

Her explanation raised more questions in Tilara's mind. What kids? Why were they at McKendree? But again she kept her wondering to herself, determined to put everything about the morning at McKendree behind her. Instead she asked, "Are you ready to go now, Aunt Clo?"

Tilara watched her aunt study her face. She saw in Cloelle's eyes a determination that mirrored her own. It made her suspicious of Cloelle's cheerful "Ready if you are!" as the two of them headed to the car.

The ride home was an undeclared battle of wills, Cloelle continuing to share information that only she was interested in, and Tilara continuing to ignore it all, except for an occasional "um" when saying nothing would have been rude.

"They're from Warren Springs—all of the kids and Dr. P."

In her silence Tilara remembered the Dr. P. story and smiled despite herself.

"March is Jimmy Jackson's boy. Jimmy and I went to school together. Braxton—he's another one of the kids—his mother was in our class, too, but she left Warren Springs years ago. One of the girls is Georgia Callaway. I knew her mother, too, but she was in the class ahead of us."

Tilara's "um" was dry and toneless.

Cloelle acted as if she didn't notice. "I don't think I know the other two kids—they call one of them Thumb, although I'm sure that's not his real name. Anyway, Dr. P. said all of them are going to be coming to McKendree on a somewhat regular basis over the summer. Not every day, but regular days during the week . . ."

"Um." Tilara used her finger to polish the shiny ridge of the window knob.

"Mr. Craighead—you remember he's the director at McKendree; I introduced you to him—well, he's giving the kids summer jobs. I don't have any idea what, and right now I don't think he does, either. But he'll come up with something. Having the kids around is a good idea. McKendree can use some young blood. . . ."

After a short silence, Cloelle's sidelong glance brought another "um."

"Anyway, Tee, I was thinking that maybe my

schedule can match the days they come. That way, while I'm working, you'll have someone to be with. They're a nice group of kids—at least the ones I know—and all around your age. They'll be going to high school this fall just like you. . . ."

Her aunt's last comment made Tilara's waiting "um" stick in her throat. What on earth could Cloelle be thinking? Asking her to spend her summer hanging around with a bunch of strange kids? Kids who knew each other and that she didn't know at all? Kids like that March, who had been at the river. Who stared at her as if she had landed from another country.

The more Tilara thought about Cloelle's suggestion, the angrier she became. All the appreciation of McKendree she had felt earlier vanished. Was this what the long-awaited summer with Aunt Cloelle was going to mean: being stuck with a bunch of strangers in a place as quiet as a tomb? Is this what was going to be better than being stuck in Boston?

Tilara continued to face stiffly forward, her speculation and anger growing. She began picking at the upholstered armrest of the door.

I might as well be listening to Papa's made-up list of summer things to do.

The force of her fingers on the fabric of the armrest tore a thread and split one of her nails. Angrily, Tilara snatched her hand away and begin nibbling on the fingernail.

If it's all the same to you, Aunt Cloelle, I'll just pick cherries or something while you go to Mc-Kendree.

Tilara glared at her aunt through a sidelong glance, then turned toward the car window. Catching a glimpse of herself in the side mirror, she unconsciously began smoothing her hair and wished she had taken more time that morning in tying it back.

But even if I had . . .

She jerked away from her image and thoughts and fell back against the cushioned seat to feel the mountain-cooled breezes on her face. Then, remembering that Cloelle had mentioned going into Warren Springs that afternoon to go shopping, she turned to her aunt and finally volunteered information.

"Sylvie asked me to go fishing with her this afternoon. If you don't mind, I think that's what I'm going to do."

Georgia and March

What's with him?

Georgia frowned as she watched March practically run to shake Mr. Craighead's hand, not even giving Dr. P. a chance to finish the introductions.

"You must be Mr. Craighead," March said, coming forward and extending his hand. "It's a pleasure to meet you, sir. I've been looking around McKendree. It's a beautiful place. I'm glad we're going to be here to help out this summer."

As March pumped Mr. Craighead's hand and grinned in his face, Georgia felt as if she were watching a bad movie. March wanted to be at McKendree even less than she did, and she knew it!

"And we're looking forward to having you," Mr. Craighead answered, patting March on the back. "Our head supervisor—Maggie Wilson's her name—will give y'all the official tour tomorrow. Still, I thought I might show you around a little today, just to give you some idea."

"Absolutely," March said, nodding his head and moving

64

beside Mr. Craighead as he led the way into the building.

Walking directly behind the director and March, Thumb mimicked the bouncy walk of the balding man who was McKendree's chief. Olivia's hand muffled her giggle, her usual show of appreciation for anything Thumb did. Braxton shook his head in disgust, his reaction to most Thumb things.

Georgia was the last one to cross the porch and walk through the door. Her green-gray eyes narrowed as she followed the others with only one thing stuck in her mind: What was March up to?

7

🌿 "This here's the sinker. It keeps the hook down in the water."

Tilara looked at the little metal piece Sylvie was pointing to on her fishing line and nodded.

"That's everything. Now you hold it."

Tilara's fingers quivered as she reached for the cane pole Sylvie held out to her, dreading what she knew Sylvie would be explaining next: how to put one of the worms on the hook. She looked down at the gray, wriggling things in the can Sylvie had brought along and whispered, "Eeee-uuuch."

Sylvie reached for the can. "What's the matter? Don't you like these worms? They nice worms— juicy and fat and ready to do some good fishing for you." Her laugh rang through the quiet glen as she pushed the can toward Tilara.

"Girl, stop!" Tilara jerked back so fast she started slipping off the large rock the two were sitting on. Sylvie grabbed for her.

"Watch it," she said, catching Tilara's arm with her free hand. She put the can of worms down beside her. "I'm just playing with you. I know you don't want to have nothing to do with these worms."

Tilara looked sheepishly at Sylvie. "I guess my secret's out, huh?"

Sylvie chuckled. "You want to fish 'bout as much as I want to get poison ivy."

"I like being here, Sylvie. It's really nice—you know, sitting by the river." Tilara picked up the pole she had dropped. "It's just that . . . um, would it be too strange for me to hold this over the water without any . . . um, fish-catching stuff on the end of it? That way I can *feel* like I'm fishing while I'm getting used to it."

The two girls looked at each other. Slow grins spread across their faces. "We'll call it fishing, city style," Sylvie said, and began baiting her hook.

Tilara reached again into the mound of dirt she had started arranging soon after they had moved back to sit on the bank. Watching her, Sylvie said, "Aren't you afraid you gonna run into one of those juicy worms while you digging in that dirt?"

Tilara giggled. "It wouldn't be the same," she said, poking her fingers into the small hill she had molded. "They would know I'm just visiting and not wanting them for sacrifice."

A flurry of birds rustled in the branches just above their heads. Tilara leaned back against the tree, enjoying the sound of the river and feel of the moist earth between her fingers.

Maybe I'll just come here while Aunt Clo is at McKendree.

Tilara's thoughts raced with reasons not to return to McKendree, to keep control of the summer ahead.

"Sylvie, do you come here a lot?"

"Every chance I get." Sylvie lowered her line deeper into the water. "Truth is, this is 'bout my best place for having some time to myself. Away from all my brothers and sisters. When Mama says I don't go nowhere, she's not counting here."

"You must catch a lot of fish."

Sylvie chuckled. "Now you going to hear one of *my* secrets. I always bring my pole with me, but I'm not always coming to fish. Sometimes I come here and just sit up against a tree like you doing."

She slowly moved her pole around in the water. "I sit here and just be quiet. Thinking mostly. Mama would call it daydreaming."

Tilara leveled and smoothed the mound of dirt. "Do you ever think about boys?" she asked.

Sylvie's eyes remained on the line that continued

to bob gently and fishless in the water. "Umhmm," she murmured. "Don't you?"

"Sometimes." Tilara traced a *T* and an *S* in the dirt. "But no one in particular." It was a half-truth, and she spoke it fast.

Sylvie slowly pulled her line toward her. "I'm not having no luck today. I might as well be trying to catch Jimmy Bradshaw."

"What?" Tilara looked up from the ground.

"Jimmy Bradshaw. He's a boy I think about in particular." Sylvia pulled in her line. "But he don't think about me."

"How do you know he doesn't?" Tilara looked back down.

" 'Cause he's the finest boy I ever seen."

Have you ever seen March Jackson?

Tilara kept her eyes on the letters she had carved into the earth.

Sylvie carefully looped her wet, empty line. "And 'cause he probably doesn't know I'm alive."

Tilara looked into Sylvie's shining, peaceful face. One she already knew she could trust. "Doesn't seem to bother you," she said after a moment.

Sylvie shrugged. "Why should I get all bothered about something I know I can't have?" she said.

Tilara picked at dirt under her thumbnail. "He's

probably not even worth thinking about. People like that are usually stuck on themselves and think everybody else feels the same way."

She heard the edge in her voice and covered it up with a grin when she looked again at Sylvie. "That's probably why you didn't catch any fish today. All the good-looking ones were too busy down there primping and stuff."

Sylvie giggled. "You really don't think about anybody in particular?" she asked.

Tilara traced her letters again, turning the *T* into the *pi* symbol and the *S* into a dollar sign. She shrugged and said softly, "Nobody."

"Nobody? Honest?" Sylvie's eyes stayed on the river.

Tilara sighed. "Not really. Sometimes Lena and I—she's my friend I was telling you about—well, she talks about boys a lot. That's when I think about them the most, I guess. When she's talking about them."

One thing for sure, I won't be wasting my time thinking about Mr. Stare-at-You-like-He's-Nuts March Jackson.

Tilara leaned back against the tree and wrapped her arms around her legs. "Maybe I'll meet ... ah, Jimmy, and we can think about him together."

"If he comes around, I'll introduce you and tell him that's what we're gonna do," Sylvia said, securing her fishing line to the pole.

Their laughter danced across the river.

8

Cloelle rushed Tilara out of the car. "You'd better hurry, sugar. We're running a little late, and I don't want you to miss Maggie's tour. I know you've already seen the place, but there's a lot . . ."

Tilara shut out the rest of what Cloelle was saying. It was bad enough that she was going to be there at all; she certainly didn't have to hear everything twice. Moving without hurrying, she got out of the car and started across the lawn.

She heard a woman's voice when she reached the porch. "Well, well, well! Isn't this what the good doctor ordered—a healthy dose of young people just itching to spend their summer at McKendree."

During the laughter that followed, Tilara slipped quietly through the screen door.

The voice of the woman filled every corner of the large room, matching its speaker. Over six feet tall, the woman was a long, proud stretch of black woman dressed in white, all the way from her snow-colored lace-up shoes to the crown of silver hair pulled back from her face and twisted into a bun that rested on the top of her head. Like a doughnut.

This picture stuck in Tilara's mind as she tiptoed in behind the group gathered in front of the woman. Maggie Wilson. *Miss* Maggie Wilson, she emphasized, introducing herself to the group.

Miss Wilson welcomed Tilara with a simple nod and smile. Tilara smiled back, relieved to be able to slip into the group without announcement. She also liked having the chance to look everyone else over before they did the same to her.

She saw that there were two girls and three boys. Standing directly in front of Miss Wilson was the boy she had met at the river.

March.

Tilara looked down at the dark wooden floor. Away from the profile.

He looks so . . . so arrogant!

Maggie Wilson continued to speak. "We're delighted you're here. Me, Mr. Craighead, and our McKendreeites." Her I'm-in-charge grin showed an even row of big white teeth.

"Well, now," she said, "follow me and we'll kill two birds with one stone. You can learn about McKendree and meet some of the residents."

As the group turned to follow Miss Wilson, Tilara saw March tap the shoulder of the boy next to him.

The tall boy. The tallest of all of them—almost eye to eye to Miss Wilson.

When the boy turned to March, Tilara saw the outline of a face whose color almost matched the thick cap of black hair above it. The high cheekbones and strong chin.

That's how an African prince must look.

Tilara could feel her breath warming in her chest.

"Man, with all the old birds in this place, that's a weird choice of words," she heard March say to the boy.

Quickly she turned away from them both, not wanting to hear the response that might come.

Only the short boy walking behind March laughed at the comment. It rippled down the long hall they were entering. The taller of the two girls looked over her shoulder and chided, "Y'all need to stop acting stupid and show some respect!"

The girl's drawl seemed extra slow, almost practiced. But it was the long, silky curls that bounced with the girl's every step that caught Tilara's attention.

When they reached the corridor, Miss Wilson held up her hand to halt the group. "We call the room we just left the great room. Its size should make it clear why it has that name. It's where you'll find our McKendreeites most afternoons and evenings after supper, sitting together, sometimes playing checkers or cards, talking, and listening to the radio."

Miss Wilson rubbed her hand up the smooth back of her tightly gathered hair. "Be sure to check there often during your days here. Take a good look around to see who you might sit and talk with. There'll usually be someone there in need of a friendly face and pleasant conversation."

"What do we talk about?"

The words were spoken so rapidly they almost ran together. Tilara turned to look at the shorter girl, who returned her look with a friendly shrug that asked, "Sounds dumb to ask, but how we supposed to know what they want to hear about?"

Tilara smiled into the friendly face with a shrug of her own in agreement.

"What's your name, dear?" Miss Wilson asked.

"Olivia," the girl said, almost blurring the four syllables.

Miss Wilson smiled gently for the first time. "It's been my observation, Olivia, that people love to talk about themselves. Especially elderly people who often live in their memories. Usually a few sincere questions about how things used to be will get the ball rolling quite nicely."

Nodding her head as a confirmation of her own response, Miss Wilson waved the group forward. They walked a few steps along the long corridor and were again motioned to stop, this time outside the first of a row of rooms.

"Most of the doors along this hall open to residents' rooms. Another corridor of rooms is on the second floor." Maggie Wilson laced her hands together as if restraining herself from pointing a finger. "Whenever you have occasion to go to a room, please remember that it is someone's home. Always knock and wait to be invited in."

"How m-m-many p-people live here, M-Miss Wilson?"

The unusually deep voice revealed itself in soft, small pieces. Tilara turned toward the sound and found herself looking into a kind face with shining black eyes. She felt heat in her face and stomach and self-consciously turned away.

"And your name, young man?" Miss Wilson asked.

"Braxton, ma'am."

Braxton.

Tilara kept her eyes on the floor.

76

"Well, Braxton, McKendree was built to house approximately seventy-five persons." Miss Wilson moved the group down the hall as she talked. "Our numbers are down now; we have only about forty-five residents."

Braxton probed further. "Are you a n-n-nurse, Miss W-W-Wilson? Are the p-p-people who work here mainly d-d-doctors and nurses?"

"To answer your first question, Braxton, yes, I'm a nurse by training. An R.N. But my title here at McKendree is head supervisor."

Maggie Wilson smoothed the collar of her starched white dress and continued. "To answer your second question, no, most of the people who work here are not health care professionals. Of course, as you know, our Dr. P. is and comes on a regular basis to check and take care of health needs. He probably told you that most of our residents are not sick. However, because they are old, they often need . . ."

While Miss Wilson's explanations continued, Tilara realized that March was looking at her. Staring. She forced herself to look back and tried to return his smile. Her face felt stiff as she did.

The group had reached a pantry-like room, a small space between two rooms with swinging doors. Tilara found herself next to Braxton.

Mmmmmm. He smells like spicy soap.

"...and so we do more visiting with our Mc-Kendreeites than actually doing things for them." Miss Wilson's voice broke into Tilara's thoughts.

"And now it's time to meet—"

Olivia interrupted just as Miss Wilson was about to push open one of the swinging doors. "Miss Wilson," she blurted in her runaway voice. "Miss Wilson, do the people here call themselves McKendreeites?"

Tilara was now close enough to see the neat side part in Olivia's red-earth hair and the deep dimples in her tan cheeks.

Miss Wilson's eyes twinkled as she responded. "To be honest, Olivia, I haven't heard anyone refer to themselves by anything other than their names." She pushed and held the door open with her hip. "And that is how I shall introduce them to you."

There were about twenty people in the squareish room they entered. Most sat at tables, a few in wheelchairs. Each table was covered with a plastic tablecloth. Scattered plates, glasses, saucers and cups, and a long buffet table with now-empty serving platters made it clear that this was the dining room.

Greetings froze in their throats as the six looked around the room. As they looked into the faces of persons who, until this minute, had not been real. Persons who up to now had been simply the old people of McKendree. McKendreeites. Now they were men and women looking back at them.

In a long moment of silence the young and old studied each other. As if something being realized had cast a spell everyone wanted to break. And so it happened all at once.

"Ladies, gentlemen—" Miss Wilson began.

"Hi, everybody—" March said.

"G-g-good morning—" Braxton started.

"My name is—" Olivia volunteered.

"Hello—" Tilara offered.

It was an off-key chorus of greetings. Then a deep bass voice rose above all the rest.

"Looka here! Look at all these pretty young folks!"

A man rose slowly from a table near the door. He used both the back of his chair and the end of the table to steady himself. His back and his legs were bent, but his head was held straight, and his smile was as welcoming as the sun.

"Mr. Reese," Miss Wilson said, "I think we should appoint you our ambassador of goodwill!"

"Don't have to have much goodwill to welcome this bunch," Mr. Reese said, slowly making his way over to the door, where they had stopped. "This group is good*ness*!"

He stopped in front of the girl whose long curls now draped over both of her shoulders. Her thin nose blushed pink against the rest of her creamy skin as a smile pushed across her face.

"What's your name, honey?" Mr. Reese said, reaching for her hand.

"Georgia," she said, lowering her lashes.

"Georgia," Mr. Reese repeated. "Gracious, gracious me. It's been awhile since a ray of prettiness like you has entered this place," he said.

"Now, Reese, don't you start your flirting with our young guests." Miss Wilson held out her arm for the old man. "And where's your cane?" she whispered, leaning close to his ear.

"I forgot it," Mr. Reese said, welcoming the additional support. "I was so anxious to get some of Miss Bertha's biscuits this morning, I forgot my extra leg."

"I can g-get it for you," Braxton volunteered hastily and then looked at Miss Wilson. "Would it b-b-be all right?"

Smiling, she nodded.

"I'd be much obliged," Mr. Reese said. "My room's on this floor. Third door down from here, on the right. While you get that extra leg, I can stay here and enjoy all this beauty."

Tilara's eyes followed Braxton as he left through the swinging door. Then they turned again to the scene in the room that now seemed transformed into lots of adoring eyes on Georgia as Mr. Reese led her farther into the room.

"Y'all com'on in here and meet the folks," Mr. Reese said, motioning to the rest of them.

As she followed with the others, Tilara looked over at Olivia, whose moving eyebrows in her direction invited conversation. For the first time in two days she began to feel that being at McKendree might turn out to be better than she had expected. She smiled in the inviting morning sun that streaked across the room, carefully keeping her eyes away from the rays bouncing on the yellow-brown curls directly in front of her.

✤ March

March gave his hair one final pat. "Perfect," he said to the image in front of him.

Staring at his reflection in the mirror on his bedroom wall, March was both pleased and puzzled. Pleased because of what he usually saw when he looked into the mirror: a body almost as big as Reggie Lomax's, the only freshman to make varsity basketball, and a face he knew girls flipped over. Puzzled because he couldn't think of one single reason why this body and face hadn't gotten to the one girl he wanted to get close to more than any other he had ever met: Tilara Haynes.

At first March hadn't thought it was strange that Tilara didn't say much. After all, that was the way shy people acted. Even the day Miss Wilson had introduced everybody around, Tilara's not saying anything to him seemed okay. But after being at McKendree as many times as they had, he could no longer say that was it. And it bothered him. Why wasn't Tilara interested in saying much to him no matter what he said to her?

Except for Olivia, Tilara didn't talk much to any of them, any of the other Real McKendreeites. March smiled, thinking about this name they had given themselves. Tilara didn't even seem interested in being friends with Georgia, and that surprised March. Georgia was popular with all the girls they hung around with in Warren Springs.

"Them girls wishing they looked like Georgia," Thumb said once when he and March were sitting out in March's yard watching a group of girls with Georgia on her porch. "You know, wishin' they was light skin and had that long, good hair."

March had laughed but hadn't said anything. Not about how much fun Georgia was to be with or how nice she always treated people. It was true that Georgia was light skinned and her hair was long and silky. His M'Dear's hair had been the same way. But his M'Dear had also been beautiful. In March's opinion Georgia would never be beautiful; she wasn't even what he called pretty. But he hadn't said any of those things to Thumb. No matter what she wasn't, Georgia was March's friend. A little while ago he had thought she might turn into a girlfriend, but now he knew that wouldn't happen. Kissing Georgia had been nice, but it hadn't made him feel *anything all that special. Nothing like he was sure it would feel kissing Tilara.*

Finally moving away from the mirror, March closed his bedroom window. His mother had reminded him three times already that rain was expected. "I hope it does rain," he muttered, pulling on the strings of the venetian blind to let it down over the window. "Then we won't have to do the walk-and-roll-the-old-folks-around-the-grounds routine Old Lady Wilson's always nagging us about."

Hearing himself made March suddenly remember something Olivia had said the last time they were on their way home from McKendree. "You know, Tilara really likes doin' stuff for those old folks," she had said, "but I'm not surprised 'cause Tilara's so nice. She's real nice."

Likes doing stuff for those old folks . . .

Hearing Olivia's words in his head again put March's thoughts into high gear.

That's it! It's time for a different approach. Time to show everybody what a nice guy I am. How absolutely devoted I am to those McKendreeites. The un-Real McKendreeites.

On his way out the door March passed the mirror again. This time, being only pleased with what he saw, he grinned and winked.

9 .

Tilara poked her head in the kitchen door. "Hi, Miss Bertha," she said.

Bertha smiled at the girl who walked through the kitchen door. One of the Kids, as she referred to the group of young people who had been coming to McKendree. The Sweet One, she called Tilara. "She treats them old folks like she's truly interested in them," Bertha said about Tilara to her niece Lauretha, who sometimes helped out in the kitchen. "Like she wants to hear what they have to say when they're sitting in there, talking like they do. And she don't mind doing some of the dirty work, neither. Lord knows I can't say that about all the Kids."

For Tilara, Miss Bertha's kitchen was almost McKendree's best place, second only to the river. There was always something simmering or baking that gave the kitchen a warming, welcoming feel and a wonderful smell. It was nothing like her kitchen at home. The only thing she felt there was Miss Katy's silent stare; the strongest smell was the scrubbing soap the housekeeper used on everything.

But what Tilara enjoyed most about the Mc-

Kendree kitchen was the sound. The sweet harmonies of Miss Bertha's gospel records, church music unlike any ever heard in the Reverend Kenneth Haynes's church. Tilara had loved the soulful sound from the first moment she heard it. It reached out to her as arms might and held her just as tightly.

Miss Bertha played her records the entire day on the wooden Victrola she kept on the table under the window. Most days she kept the music low, but sometimes Mahalia Jackson's "I Will Move On Up a Little Higher" was turned up loud enough to serenade the birds in the trees outside.

Music was playing softly when Tilara walked into the kitchen. Bertha stopped humming along to speak. "Hey there, Sweet One," she said. "How you doin' today?"

"Fine, Miss Bertha, how you doin'?" Tilara answered, pleased to hear the natural floating of her words. "Is that ginger I smell?" She moved closer to the long counter where the woman was working.

"Just opened a fresh tin of it," Bertha said. "Not even mixed in the cookie batter yet." She continued to sift the flour and tap her foot to the rhythm of the music, not missing a beat of either.

"Can I help?"

"You know anything about making ginger cookies?"

In her mind Tilara got an image of the kitchen in Boston with its industrial refrigerator and two-oven stove. Appliances needed to prepare food for church functions and big enough to bake and store a houseful of cookies. And her standing next to Miss Katy, whose frowning, pinched face made it clear that working together in the kitchen was not reasonable even to consider.

The picture made Tilara want to laugh out loud. She could almost feel the sharpness of it in her throat. "I don't know anything about making cookies at all," she said softly.

"No time like the present to learn." Bertha nodded toward the jar of molasses on the counter. "Measure me out about one-half cup," she said.

The two worked side by side at the long counter with Tilara continuing to measure out sugar, cinnamon, cloves, and lemon juice.

"You and your mama don't make cookies together?" Bertha asked. Her voice was matter-of-fact; her head continued to bob with the music.

Tilara looked over at the plump ginger-colored woman and then back to the teaspoon measure she held in her hand. "My mother's, ah . . . she's dead."

Bertha's hands were in the bowl, mixing the

dough. "My gram told me this here is the secret of truly good baking," she had said to Tilara only a minute earlier. Now she looked down at her messy hands, the only thing holding her from reaching over to touch Tilara. "Oh, Sweet One..." she began.

Hearing the sound in Bertha's voice, Tilara looked over at the woman again. "It's all right, Miss Bertha," she said. "I mean, my mother died a long time ago. Before I was two years old. I never really knew her."

"Well, I'm sorry for her and you," Miss Bertha said. "It's a shame she never got to know a daughter as sweet as you. And she had to be a lovely lady. Because only a truly lovely lady could have had such a lovely daughter."

Bertha's hands continued expertly to turn and punch the dough. "Your auntie talks about you all the time. Naturally she says what a lovely young person you are, but you know how aunties can be about their own."

Satisfied with the feel of the pastry between her fingers, Bertha removed her hands from the bowl and began wiping them off with the dish towel she always kept nearby when she cooked. "But Miss Cloelle was right," she said. "You're exactly how she said you were."

Her hands were still speckled with small bits of dough when she reached over to touch Tilara's cheek. "Truly you are."

Tilara smiled. Then, caught up in the rush of a new feeling, she reached to hug the woman. "Thank you, Miss Bertha," she said.

She turned back to the counter to finish snapping the tins shut and wrapping up leftovers. She was silent for a moment. Then, keeping her eyes on what she was doing, she said, "If my . . . if Mama hadn't died, I know we would have loved making ginger cookies together. Just like we're doing now."

Tilara turned in the direction of the back door, away from Miss Bertha's solicitous gaze. "It's about time for the others to get here," she said, moving quickly toward the door. "I'm gonna go find Olivia. I know she'll want to help roll out these cookies. We'll be back, okay?" Tilara rushed out the door and shut it behind her.

Bertha moved to the small window above the sink and strained to see beyond its corners, to catch a glimpse of Tilara and make sure she was okay. Seeing nothing, she whispered to herself, "I guess I better leave well enough alone."

Moving to her phonograph, she lifted the arm, removed the record on the turntable, and replaced it with another. Then she carefully set down the arm and turned up the volume. Strains of "I Will Move On Up a Little Higher" filled the kitchen.

Flattened against the brick wall of the small porch where she had stopped after fleeing the kitchen, Tilara stood motionless. Listening and letting the now-familiar, comforting sound wrap around her. After a moment she lifted her face toward the wind and let the waiting tears roll down her cheeks.

Not once did she try to wipe the tears away. They flowed in the embrace of the honeyed voice crooning from the kitchen and brought a healing balm. A first for her tears. Just as it had been the first time in her life that Tilara had ever thought of the woman in the everywhere pictures in the Boston house as Mama.

10

Tilara took the long way around to get to the front of the building. A route to give her time to get herself together, to make sure there were no more tears.

She was glad she had. The first person she saw was Braxton. Alone on the porch, sitting on the railing by the steps.

Braxton.

Relieved that his back was turned, she stopped in the grass, subconsciously brushing at her cheeks and patting her hair. Then she felt the familiar heat in her stomach.

Stop it.

Tilara promised herself that what had happened the last time wouldn't happen again. That the heat in her stomach wouldn't keep her from thinking of something clever to say. That when Braxton smiled, she would smile back, looking right into his face and not down at the ground.

Get yourself together!

Braxton had stepped into the center of Tilara's imagination since that first day at McKendree. He was the one she thought about most during the day and hoped to dream about at night. Sitting by Sylvie's quiet river, she traced the letters of his name in the dirt, sometimes writing her name beside his. Trying out the sound of the two names together.

Braxton and Tilara. Tilara and Braxton.

Once, in one of her letters to Lena back home, she almost said something about Braxton. How there was this boy she had met at McKendree . . . that he was so tall and had this wonderful smile . . . how really nice he was . . . that he treated the people at McKendree almost like members of his own family.

But she had decided to say nothing. For one thing she knew that Lena's questions would be endless. She could almost hear the first one: "Is he as cute as Leland Persinger?"

Braxton is nothing at all like Leland Persinger. In the first place, Braxton's human.

Keeping Braxton to herself made him even more special. Her own special, safe secret. That way no one would ask her about him—things such as what she and Braxton had said to each other or done together. Or how he felt about her.

But keeping the secret didn't stop the heat from

churning in her stomach when she was around him. And it didn't protect her now from stumbling on the bottom step when she started toward the porch.

Hearing the noise, Braxton turned around. "Hey, Tilara," he said, looking at her. "I didn't s-s-see you coming."

"Hi," she said, but the *h* caught in her throat, making the word come out sounding more like *I*.

Braxton stood up. "Looks like it's about r-r-ready to rain," he said, smiling.

"Yeah, it does." As soon as the words left her mouth, Tilara felt like kicking herself.

Can't you think of anything interesting to say?

She watched Braxton look out into the horizon and wondered if she should say how she actually liked rain—especially summer showers. Then she almost gasped when she heard her thoughts spoken out loud.

"I like rain in the s-summer." Braxton turned to Tilara. "Does that s-s-sound crazy?"

Her "Not to me, it doesn't" response was on the tip of her tongue, but before she could get it out, someone called from inside the building: March.

"Hey, folks, what's goin' on?" he said, standing at the screen door.

"Nothing, m-man," Braxton turned toward the door. "Wh-what's up in there?"

"What's up is me!" another voice said. It was Mr. Reese, partially hidden in the shadows. "And I'm wantin' to be sittin' down, as soon as possible."

Braxton seemed to cover the distance across the porch in one step. "Hey there, Mr. Reese," he said. "L-let me help you."

"I got it covered," March said. He gently kicked the screen door open.

Braxton held the door while March helped Mr. Reese across the threshold and into the rickety rocker the old man preferred. Then, pulling up a chair next to the rocker, March grinned into his face and said, "Now, Mr. Reese, how 'bout you answering that question I asked: What's goin' on?"

Tilara looked at March out the corner of her eye. It was unusual to see him being warm and friendly to the old man. She leaned back on the porch rail to watch the scene unfold.

Braxton sat on the floor in front of Mr. Reese. "Mr. Reese," he said, "w-why don't you tell us what it was like, ah, w-when you used to l-live in New York? You know, d-during the t-time of the Harlem Renaissance. Wh-what was goin' on in th-those days?"

In one of her morning chats Miss Wilson had told

them about Mr. Reese. How he had traveled all over the United States, working as a Pullman car porter. How he had usually spent his layovers in New York City—the Big Apple, Miss Wilson called it. How he had lived there during the time of the Harlem Renaissance.

Braxton had been the only one in the group who knew about the Harlem Renaissance. "A l-lot of black artists and people like that l-lived in New York then," he had volunteered. "Like L-Langston Hughes and Zora Neale Hurston. Famous w-w-writers."

Remembering this, March was determined not to be outdone by Braxton. "Yeah, Mr. Reese"—he jumped in—"what was it like to live in New York?" He cleared his throat. Making sure the new bottom of his voice stayed in place. "I'd like to hear anything you can tell us. I'm going there soon. Well, actually my whole family's going. Me, my mom and dad, my brother, Carson, and the pest, Arlene. She's my baby sister. Everybody but Rosalee, my older sister, who'll be on her way back to college." It felt good to tell about his family. March smiled and resisted the urge to steal a glance at Tilara.

Getting no comment from Mr. Reese, March continued. "It'll be great to learn more about New

York," he said. "I'll be able to tell everybody where we should go and what we should do."

Confident and satisfied with himself, March leaned back in his chair. "Yep, we'll be heading for the Big Apple, and I'm gonna be ready to take my bite."

A short moment passed as Mr. Reese enjoyed a deep chuckle. "Young man, you couldn't take a bite outta the Apple if you tried," he said, shaking his head.

"Sir?" March felt his chair wobble.

"Can't even begin to taste the Apple 'less you live there," Mr. Reese said, resting against the back of his chair. "And even if you did, there's nothin' much left for a Colored boy to chew on." He began to rock.

"Wh-what do you mean, Mr. Reese?" Braxton asked.

"I mean, New York ain't like it used to be. No, sir. That New York is gone. Maybe for all time." Mr. Reese stared into the misty distance. "Yep," he said, rocking steadily, "those days have prob'ly gone forever."

"Why d-don't you tell us about them, Mr. Reese?" Braxton said.

"Wait!" Tilara's voice came out louder than she had intended, surprising everyone, including herself. She felt heat rising in her face. "I mean, I want to hear, too. Mr. Reese, before you tell us, please wait until I go to the kitchen to find out about the ginger cookies Miss Bertha and I were making."

She could feel her words rushing together.

I sound like Olivia.

She went on. "I'll run to the kitchen to see how they're coming, and I'll get us get some lemonade while I'm there. Okay?"

March saw an opportunity and grabbed it. "Sounds good to me," he said, jumping up from his chair. "Sound good to you, Mr. Reese?"

"That would go mighty nice about now," Mr. Reese said, smiling at Tilara. "Thanks, little lady."

"I'll help you, Tilara," March said, his smile beaming. "Or, better yet, I'll go and you stay here."

"That's okay, March," Tilara said, backing up to the door. "I'll go. Miss Bertha's probably wondering what happened to me."

March reached for Tilara's arm and missed it by only a breath. As she moved, he kept his arm extended to bar her way. "Let's make a deal. We'll go to the kitchen and get the goodies, and then, Mr. Reese, you can tell us about New York City—you know, living there during the time of the, ah, the Renaissance," he said. "The good times. Right?"

"Those were good times, all right," Mr. Reese said, "but you young people don't want to be bothered with none of that stuff."

"We'd love to hear about them, Mr. Reese," Tilara said, moving out of the range of March's arm and gesturing to him that she would go by herself. "But don't get started until I get back."

"Then get to it, little lady!"

Moving much faster than usual, Tilara hurried through the door, hoping that her speed would stop March from following.

✿ M a r c h

It wasn't going at all the way he had planned. No matter what March did, nothing worked for him.

When he tried to go with her to the kitchen, Tilara had almost flown out of sight. When she came back, carrying the tray of lemonade and ginger cookies, Braxton jumped up to help before March even saw her coming. And now with Mr. Reese's long-winded stories in full swing, all March could do was just be there. Sit, listen, and be bored.

Leaning against the post at the end of the porch, March watched more than listened, thought more than heard. His only pleasure was his clear, safe view of Tilara, allowing him to take note of everything she did. How she smoothed out the hair near her left ear while she listened and usually tucked her head down whenever she was about to laugh.

And how she seemed to hang on to Braxton's every word.

What was the fascination with Braxton? His way of saying things? He remembered what Thumb said once: "Braxton thinks bein' so tall gets the girls. That ain't it. Girls think Braxton's gonna start talkin' straight when they with him. That they workin' magic on the boy."

March knew better than that. But what was it?

March studied Tilara's face as she watched Braxton ask one of his questions. How her face grew quiet as she listened. Almost as if she was waiting.

Whatever it was, Tilara's way of looking at Braxton was definitely a way she should be looking at him.

March settled in his spot against the post, his thoughts flying as he looked beyond the porch. Braxton's really into these old folks. And they return the favor. Up here he's Mr. Special.

Deep in his thoughts, March didn't notice the fly that settled on his hand. It's like when I go to Morton's . . .

The idea hit him the same moment he noticed the fly. Smiling, he brushed away one and held on to the other.

Morton's! That's where we should get together. At Morton's. We can go there next week to celebrate Thumb's birthday. Away from here. Away from all these Braxton fans.

March began to smile. Morton's. Mr. Eddie will be there. Probably H. A., too, and maybe even Tennis.

His smile grew as he thought about the regulars at Morton's. Friends of his father. Men who had known him his entire life. His fans.

Yeah. Morton's. It'll be the perfect place. Perfect!

11

The falling rain made a crystal curtain across the entire length of the long porch while the joy and laughter of the tellings—as Maggie Wilson named them that day—continued. They were bringing McKendree folks out from everywhere. Bit by bit all the spaces on the porch filled up.

Sharing his memories was giving Mr. Reese a special magic. It made his voice stronger as he continued to talk. It helped him bring alive the things he told about, making his listeners see the streets of Harlem he had known. In the music of his words they could hear the jazz sounds he claimed "stopped even birds in their tracks." The magic gave his eyes a clear, sharp roundness that kept all the other eyes fastened on his face.

Mr. Reese's magic was the spreading kind, reaching out to everyone within earshot. Such as Mrs. Richardson, who came away from the old desk in the great room for the first time in ages, holding on to Thumb's arm.

Mrs. Richardson spent the long hours of every day writing a letter to her only living relative, a niece in Memphis. Until that afternoon no one had ever seen her laugh, smile, or interrupt her letter writing for a moment. But that afternoon, swept up in the joy of the tellings, she did all three.

The magic caught hold of Mr. Marshall and Mrs. Hopson. They usually stayed in the great room all day playing double solitaire. They brought their cards with them to the porch but never got a good game started. After a while they lost interest in trying.

Olivia came outside with Miss Banks and helped her settle in on the porch swing. Miss Banks brought her knitting with her but put it down after a while. "I keep paying attention to Reese and forget where I am," she whispered to Miss Wilson, who sat down beside her. "And every time I laugh, I drop some stitches."

Georgia rolled Miss Alpha's wheelchair to the other side of Mr. Reese and sat on the porch floor next to her. The magic didn't have to reach for Miss Alpha; she felt as if she were already a part of it. As some parts of a story were told, she would lean over to Georgia and whisper a detail Mr. Reese was leaving out.

"I lived right down the street from Reese, you know," she whispered soon after she joined the group.

Mr. Reese heard and added the detail to his telling. ". . . and old Brown Skin here had an apartment with three more of her dancin' buddies. Yep, one address and four beautiful women."

103

"Reese, you ought to hush up. All that stuffin'. Shame on you!" Miss Alpha's words said one thing, but her smile and twinkling eyes said that it indeed was magic and working overtime on her.

The tellings went on as if they might never stop. Whenever Mr. Reese was about ready to wrap up one thing, someone—usually Braxton—would ask a question and get him started on another. He told about people and places, about things that had actually happened or just been planned. He covered years and brought back moments.

The magical afternoon brought a gentle joy to almost everyone. It crept right next to dinnertime as Miss Wilson moved among her McKendreeites to offer sweaters and light blankets against the chill of the late-afternoon air.

"Mr. Reese," she said, placing a blanket across his knees, "why haven't you had one of these tellings before?"

"Ain't had nobody much interested in listenin' till now." Mr. Reese cackled, brushing the blanket aside.

Then, like the rain, it was over. One after another the residents moved inside to get ready for dinner. After helping Mrs. Richardson, Tilara came back to the porch to see if anyone else needed assistance.

Everyone had gone in. The porch was empty and the lonely creak of the swing the only sound. Tilara moved across the wooden floor, picking up empty glasses, discarded napkins, and bits of unfinished ginger cookies. Things scattered here and there, behind the cracked planter near the door, under the swing with its thick, rusting chain.

This porch could use an overhaul.

It wasn't the first time the thought about McKendree's grand but shabby porch had crossed her mind, and now in the aftermath of the gathering it stayed there.

Maybe that's something we could do. . . .

Tilara stopped by one of the chairs. Its paint had completely faded.

Painting these chairs would make them like new.

She looked at the railing along the porch's edge and its uneven, cracked-paint posts.

It wouldn't be hard to fix those, either.

"We can do it!" Caught up in her own excitement, Tilara spoke her thoughts out loud. Realizing this, she giggled.

"What's so funny? Tell me so I can laugh, too."

It was March, once again coming onto the porch through the screen door.

"Nothing, really," Tilara said, bending down to pick up a glass. "I was just thinking about something."

"About what?"

Tilara could see March's feet moving closer to her as she reached for a wad of paper under the rocker.

"I was just thinking that maybe we could, um . . . that all of us could work together and, well, fix up this porch. It wouldn't be too hard if we made a plan and . . ." Tilara's voice faded as she felt her explanation rambling. She struggled to avoid March's eyes.

"Hey, that's a good idea!"

Neither of them had heard anybody else come on the porch, but Olivia's staccato fire of words was impossible to mistake.

"I wasn't tryin' to sneak up on y'all," Olivia said, walking over to them, "but I heard what you said, Tilara, and I think we ought to do it."

"Livvy, you took the words right out of my mouth." March stepped between Olivia and Tilara. "And you know what else I think?"

He moved still closer as he continued talking. "I think we should meet someplace away from here to put the plan together."

"Like, to make our plans a surprise for the Mc-Kendreeites." Olivia's voice flew with excitement.

"Yeah, something like that." March grinned. "Morton's would be a good place. I was thinking earlier that we should meet there to celebrate Thumb's birthday. We can make our ... ah, our porch plans at the same time."

He looked at Tilara. "How does that sound?" he asked.

"Sounds fine," Tilara said, moving back against the rail to put a comfortable space between herself and March.

"Perfect!" March's grin widened.

"Braxton's gonna love this idea," Olivia said. "Everybody will. Even Thumb. And it'll be fun to meet at Morton's. You been there yet, Tilara?"

Before she could answer, March jumped in. "You'll like Morton's," he said, holding back an urge to wink. "It's a great place."

Tilara's smile was weak. "Yeah," she said. "I'm sure it is."

Georgia

Watching her friends head to her bedroom, Georgia remembered the first time she had ever seen them. Theodora and Joann. She never saw one without the other. They had been together that fourth-grade year when they walked up to Georgia on the playground and Theodora asked, "Is your last name Callaway?"

It was a question right out of the blue. Neither had even spoken to Georgia before then.

"Yeah," Georgia answered. "My name's Georgia Callaway."

Theodora turned to Joann and said, "See? I told you. All them Callaways are light skinned and have straight hair, just like Gramma said." Then she grabbed Joann's hand to pull her along. "Com'on. I bet that boy over there is a Callaway, too."

Georgia had wanted to stop them, to tell them that the name of the boy Theodora was pointing to was not Callaway but Thomas. Percy Thomas. But suppose they didn't ask him what his name was. Suppose they just asked him if he was kin to her. If they did, Percy would say yes

108

because he and Georgia were cousins. His mother and Georgia's mother were sisters.

Georgia had stood there on the playground, watching Theodora talking to her cousin Percy. She saw Percy pointing to her, and in her mind she could hear the tall girl saying again, "See, I told you."

Standing there on the playground, Georgia thought about her family in a way she never had before. About how they all looked crowded together around the table in Nana's dining room at Thanksgiving. How all of Nana's children looked almost white. Like Aunt Lydia, Percy's mother, who had married Raymond Thomas, a man almost as light skinned as she. Like her own mother.

That evening after supper Georgia had pulled out the family album Nana kept in the bottom drawer of the big cabinet in the dining room. The china closet, Nana called it. While Nana hummed in the kitchen, Georgia sat at the big table and looked through the plastic-covered pages filled with pictures of Callaways. Young, old, living, no-longer-living, and married-to Callaways.

"Every time I see that picture of your mother I want to laugh." Nana's voice right behind her made Georgia jump. She hadn't heard her grandmother come into the room.

"That picture there." Reaching over Georgia's shoulder, Nana pointed to a picture of a young girl looking directly into the camera and sticking out her tongue. It was a picture of Esther Callaway, Georgia's mother, when she was nine years old.

"Esther always did have a lot of spunk." Nana traced the pictures on the page gently with her finger. "But then, all the Callaway children have something special," she said.

Georgia turned to look at her grandmother. The look she saw on Nana's face was the same she had seen when Georgia had won first place in the essay contest at school. A look of pride.

"Just like you have something special, my Georgia girl," her grandmother had said, giving Georgia a shoulder hug.

Was that "something special" looking like all the other Callaways? Georgia had never quite figured this out. She used to wonder about it, but as the years passed, it didn't seem to matter much. The simple truth was, Georgia did look like all the other Callaways. And that was that.

Now, waiting for Theodora and Joann so she could convince them to go to Morton's with her, Georgia examined her reflection. She hoped this time Joann wouldn't stare at her as she sometimes did when the two of them sat together in front of the mirror. Looking into her own green-gray eyes, Georgia remembered something Nana had said once about Joann. "You know, that Joann's a pretty little thing, even being as dark as she is."

Brushing the back of her hair one more time, Georgia wondered out loud. "Hmmm . . . I should tell Joann what Nana said. That's probably just the thing she needs to hear."

12

꧁ Morton's Drugstore.

Tilara sat in the car, staring at the sign, an ordinary sign with flashing lights around it, hanging above a door.

As she looked at it, she struggled to get through the cloud that seemed to be sitting in front of her thoughts. Like something to keep her from seeing a picture in her mind, to keep her from making connections.

Something similar had happened the first time she and Cloelle had come to Warren Springs. Riding along the streets and listening to her aunt point out this thing and that, Tilara felt as if she were riding through one of her own dreams. Everything the car passed was something she could almost remember. Almost, but not quite. Things almost familiar but still strange.

And now this sign. Morton's Drugstore.

Cloelle's voice seemed far away but broke through her thoughts. Tilara pulled her eyes away from the sign and looked at her aunt. "Huh? I mean, what did you say, Aunt Clo?" she asked.

"I said, from the way you're staring, you must be remembering the taste of that ice-cream soda," Cloelle repeated.

"Ice-cream soda?" Tilara frowned.

"Your very first," Cloelle said, chuckling. "Chocolate, with chocolate ice cream. I can still remember the look on your face when you took that first sip."

Part of the cloud moved away. A corner of the picture cleared.

Tilara saw herself sitting on her knees in a booth, making herself taller. That way she could look down on the shimmering brown foam rising above the tall, thick glass. Kneeling made her high enough to put her lips on the very tip of the straw floating next to the long silver spoon she could use to dig into the glass.

"Kenneth got such a kick out of seeing you tackle that soda," Cloelle said, chuckling again.

Another corner of memory cleared. Tilara could hear her father's laughter as he used his big white handkerchief to wipe away the deliciously sticky chocolate she felt around her mouth. "You better get vanilla next time, baby girl," he had said, "to make it easier for me to see where your face needs cleaning up."

Suddenly the entire picture in her mind was as clear as the sign above the drugstore door. The sign she had seen across the shoulder of the girl with the china white, baby-doll face when the girl came through the door, holding the hand of a woman who had the same face.

Her father had stood up. "Well, look who's here," he said, hugging the china white, baby-doll woman. "Is this your baby, Esther? Of course it is, looking just as pretty as you."

Tilara remembered moving off her knees and sitting back down on the seat of the booth. Moving into the shadow of her father's back and away from the green-gray eyes of the little girl whose yellow ribbon had slipped almost to the end of one long silky curl.

The girl looked at her mother. "I want a ice-cream soda, too, Mama," she said. "I want vanilla with vanilla ice cream and two cherries on top!"

Tilara squeezed her eyes shut to cut the picture away. But when she opened them, the sign was still there.

Morton's Drugstore.

"Should I pick you up here or at one of your friends' houses?" her aunt asked. "I'm at your service, ma'am."

"Here will be fine, Aunt Clo," Tilara said, reaching for the handle of the door. "And I'll be ready whenever you get back from shopping."

Slowly she got out, shut the door, and made her way from the safety of the car.

13

The first thing everyone noticed when walking into Morton's was the smell. Lady Mary, who owned the drugstore with her husband, Eddie, called it a salad smell. "Everything mixes together, but nothing loses its special scent," she would say.

The smell of the medicines Mr. Eddie measured to fill prescriptions mixed with the chocolate, butterscotch, and cherry syrups Miss Anna poured over ice cream to make sundaes. The hot dogs on the grill mixed with the perfumes Lady Mary tried out on her wrists so she could describe them to customers. And the smell of H. A.'s cigar mixed with everything.

The smell of Morton's was something people remembered whenever they came back to the store. Even if years passed between the first and next times. Tilara found this out as soon as she opened the heavy oak and glass door. The smells caught hold of her and took her on another spin through time.

"Tilara! Hey," March called. He was standing with Braxton and a group of men.

"Hi, March," Tilara said. "Hi, Braxton." She was relieved to hear her voice sound normal. She didn't feel normal at all.

Afraid that her legs would shake if she walked, she remained by the door and looked around, matching what she saw with what she remembered.

The wood shelves lining the entire side of one wall still climbed all the way to the ceiling, each crowded with bottles and jars in every size, shape, and color. Two glass cases still made an L in front of the door the white-jacketed pharmacist went in and out of. The comic-book and magazine racks were still beside the jukebox that didn't light up, and a scale that did was still beside the jukebox. The marble soda-fountain counter was still to the left of the door, and the glass-topped tables with their heart-shaped chairs were still to the right. And the row of wooden booths still lined the aisle leading to the back.

Tilara felt as if she had walked through a mirror, going back in time. She began to feel light headed and reached out for the door handle to keep herself from falling.

"Tilara, are you all right?"

March was standing in front of her. Tilara hadn't even noticed him coming close.

"Tilara?" he asked again.

As she began to speak, Tilara realized that she had been holding her breath. A great rush of air came out before her words.

"I'm fine," Tilara said, forcing herself to smile at March and not look into those honey-gold eyes. "I just . . . ah, I mean, it seems like . . ." She couldn't decide what to explain.

"It seems like no place you've ever seen before, right?" He smiled. "We all say that about Morton's. We keep tellin' Mr. Eddie and Lady Mary that, too, but—"

Another memory picture came to life. "Lady Mary . . ." Tilara whispered her thought aloud.

"Yeah," March was saying. "She and Mr. Eddie own Morton's." March leaned close as he continued speaking softly. "Mr. Eddie started calling his wife the Lady even before they got married. After they hooked up, he kept on callin' her that, and it just caught on. Now practically everybody calls her Lady. Sometimes she even calls herself that."

March looked into Tilara's face and winked. "There're good stories everywhere, not just on that old porch at McKendree," he said. "H. A. was just telling everybody about—"

"H. A.?" Tilara said, her voice reflecting the blur of the things she was seeing and hearing.

March laughed. "Oh, yeah," he said. "I'd better tell you that story, too. Especially since you're about to meet him."

Deciding that this wasn't a good time to take her hand, March pointed in the direction he wanted Tilara to go. As the two headed to the group that included Braxton, March's whispers explained how the man's name was Mr. Clarence Ray and that "H. A." stood for "house arrest." How it was the name given to the cigar-smoking man by his wife, who told everybody that the only way to keep her husband from hanging out at Morton's would be to put him under "house arrest."

March touched the arm of the man he stopped beside. "Excuse me, Mr. Lewis," he said. "I want y'all to meet Tilara."

A tall man who had Braxton's face looked down at Tilara and smiled. "Tilara," he repeated in a deep voice. "You must be the Tilara my son has talked about."

The words swept over Tilara.

Braxton's talked about me. He's told his father about me.

The smile on her face reflected her thoughts.

Braxton was standing next to his father. He grinned at Tilara. "Hey, again, T-Tilara," he said.

"And this is Mr. Ray, who everybody calls H. A."
March pointed to the man who had been talking.
He was holding the biggest cigar Tilara had ever
seen.

"And exactly what is Miss Tilara's last name?"
H. A. asked, extending his hand to Tilara.

"Haynes," she answered, shaking his hand.
"Tilara Haynes."

"Haynes? Did you say Haynes?"

Turning to see who the speaker was, Tilara found
herself looking into a face under a halo of curly
white hair, a face she felt she had seen before.

"Yes, ma'am," Tilara said, liking the face and
searching her memory to place it.

"Are you Kenneth Haynes's girl?" the speaker
said, putting her hand under Tilara's chin.

"Yes."

"I knew it!" the woman said, taking great pleasure in her discovery. She put her arm around
Tilara. "Eddie," she said, "this is Kenneth's daughter. You remember Kenneth Haynes."

The last person from the group to be introduced
to Tilara walked over to stand beside the sweet-
faced woman. "Course I do," he said. "How I'm
gonna forget that character?"

The man looked at Tilara and smiled. "Well, I

120

declare," he said. "Kenneth's baby. I haven't seen your daddy in ages. How is he? Is he here in town with you?"

"No, sir," Tilara said. "I came alone. I mean . . . I'm visiting my aunt, but she doesn't live here anymore. She lives in the valley, near Mount Hope."

"Cloelle!" The woman smiled with another discovery. "Cloelle Haynes."

"Yes," Tilara said. Her mind raced with wonder about this woman who knew so much about her family.

"I should have known who you were as soon as I laid eyes on you, baby," the woman said. "You have Haynes written all over you."

At that moment the door opened, and Georgia, Olivia, and two other girls Tilara didn't know walked in. "Hey, everybody," they said.

During the chorus of greetings Tilara had her own salad of feelings. Some were hot, and some cold; some were hard, and others soft. They came one after another, and they all mixed together.

You have Haynes written all over you.

As her thoughts pounded in her head, Tilara found herself staring at Georgia, whose green dress reflected the color of her eyes and whose pulled-up long curls framed her face and kissed her shoulders.

Georgia, who seemed to be surrounded by the men of Morton's. All smiling. All admiring.

You have Haynes written all over you.

The picture of herself Tilara carried inside flashed across her mind's eye. Tilara Haynes. Dark like all the Hayneses. Like her father and Aunt Cloelle. Like her great-aunt Diane, who had been the last to live in the Haynes family home. Like all the Hayneses with their tight curly hair. "Comb-challenging stuff," her father once said.

You have Haynes written all over you.

Tilara turned her head, wanting to wipe away every picture—the ones she could actually see and the ones she imagined. Her eyes rested on Olivia's face, which, as usual, wore a smile.

"Thumb'll be here in a minute," Olivia said. "Com'on, let's get that back booth. It'll be big enough for everybody."

By the time Thumb came, they were seated in the booth and looking over the one-page paper menus.

"Where you been, man?" March said, moving closer to Georgia to make room for Thumb. "This is your party, and you're late."

"Man," Thumb said, shaking his head, "my

mama makes me crazy. She found so much stuff for me to do, I wanted to lock her in a closet."

Georgia laughed. "Thumb, if you *really* want your mama to make you crazy, you just try lockin' her in a closet."

"Can't you just see Miz Martin locked in a closet and Thumb standing by the door with the key in his hand...." Olivia said, her eyes twinkling as she laughed.

"Yeah," said Braxton, "and a t-t-train t-ticket in the other."

"Y'all terrible," Thumb said, unable to hold back his own laughter. "But sho *nuff* tellin' the truth. My mama would follow me to the ends of the earth to wear my behind out!"

March noticed that Tilara kept her eyes on the menu. "Tilara," he said, leaning across the table to look directly into her eyes. "Was your dad following someone to the ends of the earth? Is that why he moved so far away from here?"

"What?" Tilara looked up from the menu, surprised at the question and not knowing what to say.

"Your daddy used to live here, Tilara?" Thumb asked.

"Yes, he did—" Tilara began.

"You should have gotten here on time, Horace,"

March said, teasing Thumb with the use of his given name. "Then you'd know that Tilara's father grew up here *and* went to school with my dad and Georgia's mom."

March made no effort to hold back his grin. It was going to be a great away-from-McKendree day.

"Lady Mary knew who Tilara was as soon as she laid eyes on her," he went on. "She knows the family so well she could see Haynes written all over Tilara. Isn't that right, Tilara?" He looked at Tilara, who he had made certain would be seated directly across from him in the spacious booth.

Tilara was holding the menu so tightly her fingers almost pressed clear through the thin sheet. "Umhmm," she murmured, looking at the handwritten list of treats.

A soft, slow voice fell over the group. "Y'all decided what you want?" It was Miss Anna, coming beside the booth to take the orders.

"You don't even have to ask me, Miss Anna," Georgia said, handing her menu to the round-faced woman who was famous for her delicious fountain concoctions. "I'll have the same as always: a vanilla ice cream soda with vanilla ice cream. And, Miss Anna, can you please put two cherries on top?"

March and Braxton

March turned and curved his body to the rhythms of the music coming from the radio on a nearby porch. The street-lamp above him outlined a shadow in graceful motion.

"Make up your mind, man," he said to Braxton. "Are you comin' to the Youth Center or not?"

"Yeah, I g-g-guess so," Braxton answered, "b-but I don't want t-to stay out t-t-too late."

"Don't worry, we won't," March said, mimicking the movements of a tap dancer. "Anyhow, tomorrow's Sunday."

"What's th-that got to d-d-do with anything?" Braxton's shadow next to March's was long and still.

"No McKendree. You can sleep late." March's right foot matched the steady beat of the drum.

"I promised Pops I'd go to church with him," Braxton said.

The record ended. March rested his tapping foot with a flourish. "Man, you gotta get with it," he said. "I haven't gone to church once since we been goin' to McKendree. I convinced Jimmy and Marilyn that I need at least one day to catch up on my rest."

"Man, you g-g-get away with more stuff with your parents. My p-pops wouldn't buy that even if I gave him the m-money."

The two friends laughed together and continued down the softly lit summer street.

"Hey, Miz Redd, Mr. Redd!" March and Braxton waved to the couple sitting on their porch.

"How you doin', boys?"

"Joann at the center?" March asked.

"She is," the woman said, "and when you see her, remind her that we're expecting her home by ten."

"Yes, ma'am." March waved again. "See y'all later."

"If J-Joann's there, p-p-probably wild-mouth Th-Theodora is, too," Braxton said as they moved on down the street.

"Yeah, you never see one without the other." March chuckled.

A block away the noise of the music and kids at the center reached out and rushed their steps.

"Too bad Tilara couldn't stay in town," March said.

Braxton kicked away a small stone in his path.

"Said she had to head on home with her aunt," March said, a frown above his narrowed eyes.

126

He shoved his hands in his pockets as Tilara's protests replayed in his mind. Her tone and voice had been strong when she insisted that she couldn't join the rest of them at the center that night. Even when Olivia volunteered a free ride in her father's taxi as a means of getting back to Cloelle's valley home, Tilara remained set on leaving.

"T-too bad. T-Tilara's nice. So's her aunt, Miss Haynes."

"Yeah." March nodded.

The picture of Tilara sitting in Morton's drifted through his mind. Sitting across from him in the crowded booth with her neat scoop of vanilla ice cream covered with only a few splashes of chocolate syrup. Miss Anna had questioned Tilara about her order.

"You just want your ice cream plain, baby? Don't you want anything on it?"

"Well, maybe a little chocolate syrup," Tilara answered. "But just a very little."

The noise of traffic signaling the nearby intersection slowed their steps.

"How come Georgia d-didn't want to come?" Braxton wondered aloud, his eyes on the sidewalk.

"Who knows?" March brushed his hand over his hair. "She's been actin' a little strange these days."

"How?" Braxton looked at March.

"Just strange." March shrugged his shoulders again. "Who knows what gets into girls' heads? Not me."

They waited on the street corner for the oncoming cars to pass. The noise and music beckoned louder.

"All I know is, it's time to party! Com'on, man, let's get to it!"

The two friends loped across the clear street, past the darkened Morton's sign to the crowded Youth Center next door.

14

Mick Morris laid his carefully folded napkin next to his empty plate. "That was as fine an apple pie as I've ever had! My compliments to the baker," he said, smiling at Tilara.

"Thank you, Mr. Morris." Tilara bowed her head demurely.

Over the summer Tilara had looked forward to Mr. Morris's visits, especially their relaxing Sunday afternoon dinners. Mr. Morris wasn't like most adults, who managed to question, examine, pick at, and ignore you at the same time. He seemed sincerely interested in what she had to say and didn't go after things she left unsaid.

She also enjoyed seeing her aunt and Mr. Morris together. Watching the two talk over coffee or laugh at the drive-in theater made it easy to picture herself with someone she cared about the way Cloelle cared about Mick Morris.

Braxton.

In the privacy of her imagination Tilara saw Braxton there at the table, laughing and talking with her as Mr. Morris was doing. Watching Mick Morris, she conjured Braxton's actions, taking a pipe from his jacket pocket and tapping it against the ashtray.

"I hear you went in to Warren Springs yesterday," Mr. Morris said, filling his pipe with fresh tobacco. "Did you have a good time?"

Tilara shrugged her shoulders. "It was okay," she said.

Cloelle came into the dining room, carrying a pot of coffee. "You never did finish telling me about being at Morton's, Tee," she said, clearing a place for the percolator.

"Nothin' much to tell," Tilara said, shrugging. "We just had ice cream and stuff and talked."

In the silence that followed, Cloelle began pouring the coffee. "You'll never guess who I saw coming out of Morton's when I came to pick Tilara up," she said, handing a cup to Mick.

"Who?"

"Clarence Ray," Cloelle said. "Better known as H. A., of course."

Mr. Morris carefully measured a teaspoon of sugar into his coffee. "Good old H. A.," he said, chuckling. "What's that rascal up to?"

"Same old H. A.," Cloelle said, drizzling cream into her cup. "I asked him the same thing, and he told me he was working on his second million."

"His *second* million? When did he get the first?"

"That's what I wanted to know," Cloelle said, holding up her cup and blowing across the steaming liquid. "He said he had given up on the first and decided to just go on and get the second."

The three of them laughed. The hint of uneasiness that had been there earlier passed from the room.

"Some things will never change, and H. A. is one of them," Mr. Morris said.

"Yep," Cloelle agreed, "and you can count on him to be at the heart of a good conversation. From what he said, yesterday's argument was about whether or not Morton's should have moved from uptown."

"From uptown?"

"You remember, Mick," Cloelle said, adding a sprinkle of sugar to her coffee. "Morton's used to be in a building off Main Street, right in the heart of the uptown area. That's where it was when I was a little girl."

"Now, Cloelle, you know that was before my time." He winked at Tilara.

Cloelle rolled her eyes. "You wish," she said. "Anyhow, Morton's was one of several Negro businesses forced to move from the uptown area

when that entire commercial district began booming."

"They were talking about that yesterday," Tilara
said. She grabbed her spoon and held it up as if it
were a cigar. Then she puffed out her cheeks to give
herself an H. A. look. " 'We should have protested;
that's exactly what we should have done. We should
be setting examples for our young folks instead of
standing around here talking smoke. 'Cause that's
exactly what we doing. Talking smoke!' "

Cloelle and Mick Morris shrieked with laughter.
Tilara's mimicking of H. A. was flawless.

"That's H. A. all right," Mick said, still laughing.
"He's a character."

"How do you know H. A., Mr. Morris?" Tilara
asked.

"The same way I know all those drugstore
philosophers," he said. "The same way I know
Cloelle."

"Most of us went to high school together,"
Cloelle explained. "Mick was in my class just like
March's dad was in your father's. March is Jimmy
Jackson's son," she added, looking at Mick.

"Jimmy Jackson," Mr. Morris said, stroking his
neat mustache. "He took over his father's store after
the old man died, right?"

"And his son March is the old man reincarnated."

Cloelle looked at Tilara over the rim of her cup as she sipped her coffee. "March is one fine-looking young man, wouldn't you say?" she said.

"He's okay." Tilara busied herself brushing crumbs from around her plate into her hand.

Cloelle raised her eyebrows as she looked at Mick Morris out the corner of her eye. "I think just about every female at McKendree has noticed that cleft in his chin. I know *I* have." Cloelle winked at Mick.

Tilara dumped the crumbs from her hand onto her plate. "Aunt Clo," she said, "you sound like Olivia. She's always sayin' how every girl in their class is after March. She says all the girls want to go with March. . . ." Tilara snickered. "And all the boys want to go with Georgia Callaway."

"Callaway?" Mr. Morris frowned slightly, looking into the air. "That name rings a bell."

"I'm sure it does," Cloelle said, smiling over the rim of her coffee cup. "I *know* you remember Georgia's mother, Esther Callaway."

Mick chuckled. "Lord, Cloelle, how on earth do you remember that?" He rested against the back of his chair and stretched out his legs. "Miss 'light, bright, and damned near white' Esther," he said. "I think all us fellows were in love with that girl."

Tilara watched her aunt and Mr. Morris laughing together and felt a new heat rising from her stomach.

"You know, Tilara," Mr. Morris said, reaching for the coffee, "in our day it seemed like every colored boy wanted a girl like Esther on his arm, and I guess I was no different."

"The whole bunch of you fawned over Esther like she was a piece of gold." Cloelle put her hand on the coffeepot, testing its warmth. "I can remember Mama telling me practically every day how pretty I was, trying to convince me that it was okay to be the color of a Hershey chocolate bar."

Tilara felt the heat reach her throat. It began pushing out her thoughts even as she tried holding them in. "Aunt Cloelle, was Grandma Haynes trying to convince Papa, too? 'Cause if she was, she failed."

Both Mr. Morris and Cloelle looked at Tilara. Her tone was one they had not heard before.

Tilara's hot words had surprised even her. But they kept coming. "I bet Papa was like that about my mother. The way Mr. Morris was over . . . over that Esther Callaway. I think Papa was convinced that light-skinned girls are prettier."

Cloelle had clasped the handle of the pot, preparing to take it into the kitchen to warm the coffee. But she did not move from her chair. "What makes you think that, Tee?" she asked softly.

"I just do," Tilara said, her eyes again on the tablecloth. "Just like I think that a lot of people *still* think being light skinned is better."

Tilara reached for the coffeepot. "I'll warm that up, Aunt Clo," she said, getting up from the table and continuing to talk as she went into the kitchen. "All I know is, a lot of folks act like . . . I mean, they, well, you know, they make over people like Georgia. And it's not just here, either. There's this girl at school. Cynthia Gordon. She's like Georgia . . . you know, light with straight hair and all. Mrs. Henry, who was our homeroom teacher, she always acted like Cynthia Gordon was the only person on the planet with good sense."

In another imitation Tilara made her voice high and whiny. " 'Cynthia, do this. Cynthia, you're so this. Cynthia, Cynthia, Cynthia.' " Tilara sucked her teeth. "Cynthia's an okay person, I guess," she said in her normal tone. "But it would be hard to know it from the way Mrs. Henry carried on."

A noisy silence fell as Tilara stood in the kitchen doorway, waiting for the plugged-in coffee to warm. Then Cloelle's voice reached across the room.

"Tee," she said, "what was Mrs. Henry's attitude toward you?"

Tilara felt the heat in her face. In her cheeks, her ears. It made her mouth feel dry. "What do you mean, Aunt Clo?" she asked.

"Just what I said. What was the teacher's attitude toward you?"

Suddenly it was time to realize a very old anger in a brand-new way. There and then. It was safe. Love she could trust surrounded her. More than enough to give her power.

The words of Miss Bertha's song played in her head.

. . . move on up a little higher . . .

Tilara took a deep breath. "I know I shouldn't care what Mrs. Henry's attitudes are. About me or anything else. She's not anything to me. She's just a teacher that I won't ever have anymore. So it would be stupid to care what she thinks. People like her are gonna think what they want anyway, no matter what. They follow after things because of dumb reasons."

Tilara turned away as the heat reached her eyes and brought a feeling of tears. "But what's really, *really* dumb," she said, fighting to keep the tears out of her voice, "is knowing that and caring anyway."

In the few minutes that passed before Tilara

came out of the kitchen, a cloud of quiet wrapped Cloelle and Mick. Both wanted to say something to Tilara but at the same time felt she had begun to say it for herself. When she finally came back carrying the steaming coffee, they saw the first break of a smile on her face, and they knew.

"But I'm learning," she said quietly.

"Well, I should hope so," Mick Morris said. "Maybe soon you'll be almost as smart as me."

Resting back in his chair, Mick proceeded to relight his pipe. "If not, at least smart enough to know that you, my dear, like your aunt, are downright lovely, whether you want to hear that fact or not." His deep, warm voice was filled with heart.

A smile began to bloom on Tilara's face. First it widened her lips; then it moved to her eyes and danced there.

"Mr. Morris," she said, "I think you're beginning to sound a little like Grandma Haynes. Are you telling me it's okay to be the color of a Hershey chocolate bar?"

"Like I said, child," he said, breaking into a big grin, "I don't like to waste my time tellin' folks things they ought to already know." He pulled his chair closer to the table. "Now, how about sharing some of that hot coffee?"

Tilara refilled the cups, first her aunt's and then Mr. Morris's.

"Tilara, won't you join us with a cup?" he said, carefully spooning in sugar.

Tilara put the coffeepot back on its hot pad on the table. "No, thanks," she said. "I really don't like the taste of coffee. And anyhow . . ." Tilara's words were lost in her giggles.

" 'Anyhow' what?" Cloelle asked.

"I was just thinking about Miss Alpha and what she said one day when I brought some coffee to her and Mr. Reese." Tilara sat back down. "Now that I think about it, Miss Alpha was doin' a Mrs. Henry. And I bet anything that Miss Alpha believes what she said is actually true."

"So what did she say?" Mick asked.

"Miss Alpha said," Tilara began, and then took on the high-pitched voice of the old woman, " 'Why, darlin', I *never* drink coffee, and you shouldn't, either. Coffee makes you black, you know.' "

For a moment only the fading sun shadows filled the small dining room. Then the laughter of Tilara, Cloelle, and Mick Morris rang out to welcome the darkness creeping down from the hills nearby.

15

Tilara's loud sigh caused Tut to mew a protest before jumping off her lap. She reached down to stroke the cat's soft gray head. "Sorry, Tut," she murmured. "I'm trying to decide what news I have for Papa this week."

Tut stared into Tilara's face as if offering a suggestion of his own. His look made her giggle. "Oh, yeah, I can tell him about you," she said, reminded that she and Cloelle had taken in the tiny stray only a few days ago, several days after last week's phone call to her father.

The Sunday night long-distance call to Boston had become a summer ritual, one Tilara did not especially look forward to. It wasn't that she hadn't missed her father or didn't want to talk to him. It was just that . . .

I don't have to talk to Papa to know exactly what he's going to say. He always says the same thing.

Even in her mind Tilara could hear her father's deep, authoritative tones.

Tell me, Tilara, what did you do interesting this

week? And may I assume that you're keeping up with your reading?

Tilara bent to pick up Tut, thinking how she would like to answer her father the next time he asked that question.

Well, Papa, I've been reading this romance magazine I got from my friend Sylvie, and, Papa, you just can't imagine all the stuff I'm reading about!

She couldn't keep from giggling as she stroked Tut behind his ears. Once again Tut found the sound irritating and leaped from her lap.

"Oh, Tut, you're as particular as Papa!" She poked at the cat with her toe. "Stay there on that hard floor and see if I care. I've got a call to make anyhow."

Instead of the 0 needed to place a long-distance call, Tilara found herself dialing 9631, Sylvie's number.

I'll call Papa later.

She and Sylvie decided to walk to the gas station on the highway near Cloelle's house. Tilara liked going there to get pop out of the machine. She enjoyed searching the big metal chest for the special flavor she wanted. It would be mixed in with all the other sodas lined up in the cooler, all of them hanging between the long silver strips. She liked feeling the cold wetness on her hands while she moved the bottles around to get the one she wanted. She hadn't seen pop machines like this in Boston.

Walking back home, she and Sylvie started catching up with each other. It had been almost a week since they had been together, and as usual Sylvie had something new to tell her.

"This boy—his name's Aaron, I think. Anyway, he's Lucille's cousin—you met her that time when we went to church, remember? He's from Atlanta and visitin' here for the summer. Girl, I saw him down at the filling station, and he is *too* fine! Finer than Jimmy Bradshaw. Lucille said he was, and for once she knew what she was talkin' about. Some of the time Lucille's taste ain't nowhere but in her mouth, but this time she hit the nail on the head."

Listening, Tilara smiled, enjoying Sylvie and the cool, delicious soda.

"So, where'd y'all go yesterday?" Sylvia asked when she finished the account of Lucille's cousin. "Me and my sister Verdell started over to your house, but when we didn't see Miss Cloelle's car, we turned back."

"We went to Warren Springs." Tilara rolled her

tongue in the last remaining sip, hanging on to the prickly feel of the bubbles.

"Did you go shopping?"

Tilara shook her head. Swallowing, she said, "Nope. We just . . . just hung around."

"That's what me and Verdell ended up doin'. Only we did it at home. I bet you had more fun hanging than me."

The two girls giggled together as they continued along the tree-lined path.

In the air filled with the familiar night songs, Sylvie began to sing softly.

"Walking through here at night makes me think of that song," she said to Tilara. "You know the one I mean?"

"Umhmm." Tilara nodded her head. " 'Nature Boy.' I love that song. Especially the way Nat King Cole sings it."

"Me, too," Sylvie said, "even though it is kind of sad."

"Not to me." Tilara picked up the melody and hummed along.

The feeling of wanting to talk about Braxton swept over her. He came into her mind every time she heard the song.

I've just got to tell somebody!

Now would be the time. She would tell Sylvie. The words formed in her mind.

There's this boy at McKendree ... that song makes me think of him.

But before she could get the words out, Sylvie spoke.

"Oh, yeah, there's something I been meaning to ask you about. Mama said that Miss Bertha— remember how you were tellin' me about Miss Bertha, and I told you that Mama knew her? Well, Miss Bertha was tellin' Mama about this boy who comes with y'all to McKendree. Mama said Miss Bertha was sayin' how fine he is. Somebody named, ah ... named something like a month, Mama said."

Tilara's waiting words faded as the lovely melody lost itself in the night.

"Who she talkin' about, Tilara?" Sylvie kept on. "And how come you never told me about him?"

Tilara kicked at a stick along the path. "Nothing to tell," she said.

"But who's Miss Bertha talkin' about?" Sylvie insisted.

"Probably March," Tilara said, her voice flat.

"Is he all that fine? And if he is, how come you never said anything about him?"

Fine. Always worrying about somebody being fine. So what? Who cares?

143

Tilara wanted to say her thoughts out loud. But instead she said, "Sylvie, there's a real easy way for you to find out everything about McKendree you ever wanted to know."

"How's that?"

"Come there with me. I'm going Monday. Tomorrow."

Sylvie's laugh was shy, a little nervous. "I can't," she said. "I got too much to do, helping Mama and everything."

"But your mama said she wanted you to get out more, to be around people your own age. Remember?"

Tilara heard the challenge in her own voice. Frowning at herself, she hurried to soften her words. "It's fun at McKendree, Sylvie. Really. You'd be surprised. And we can use all the help we can get for our next project. We're going to fix up the front porch."

"Girl, I get enough fixing-up stuff to do at home. If that's the fun y'all havin' at McKendree, you can leave me out."

There had been a slight edge in Sylvie's voice. For a moment both of them were silent; then Tilara moved the conversation someplace else.

"Aunt Clo and Mr. Morris said something about going to the drive-in. If they do, want to come?"

"Yeah," Sylvie said, her voice light again. "I love going to the drive-in and don't even care what's playing."

Tilara laughed. "Me, either."

Glad to see the uncomfortable moment pass, Tilara grabbed Sylvie's hand and pulled her along the darkening glen.

McKendree

To some it might have looked like a hubbub. But not to Maggie Wilson. She knew exactly what it was, even though that was the word she used when she climbed out of Dr. P.'s car.

"Gracious me. It's a hubbub!"

And knowing made her heart sing as she looked across the broad green lawn and took in everything she saw.

A hubbub.

Working alongside Tilara were Miss Banks, Mrs. Hopson, and Mrs. Richardson. Each of the elderly women was helping to plant a border of chrysanthemums to line the asphalt path leading to the building. Tilara's words of praise and support floated above the group.

"Those two colors go good together, Mrs. Hopson."

"Hold on, Mrs. Richardson. I'll move that pot for you."

On the porch March was making a final check of the tightened pegs in the railing, and Braxton was smoothing the last rough edges of the floorboards. Mr. Reese was directing their efforts from his rocking chair, which had been moved down to a level place on the grass.

146

"Look at that post over there, young fella. Can't you see how it's wobblin'? Watch it, boy! You gonna pound your fingers into the porch handlin' a hammer like that!"

Olivia sat on a blanket near the rhododendron bushes with the group of pillow makers she had recruited. Along with four of the residents, Miss Bertha had become a part of this group after she had brought out iced tea and sugar cookies for everybody. All of them stitched the pillows that would eventually be placed on the newly repaired porch furniture.

Joining Thumb and Georgia to paint the furniture were Mr. Marshall and Mr. Jeffries. Georgia had been the first to dip a brush into Thumb's careful mixture and was spreading color on one of the faded wicker pieces while Thumb called words of encouragement to his crew.

"Com'on, Mr. J., that table is just waiting for you to make it pretty. Don't forget, y'all. Everybody gets to put their initials on the pieces they paint."

"Yes, indeed," Dr. P. murmured. "A hubbub in the name of loving!"

16

"This place looks good!"

Thumb stood at the bottom of the steps, admiring his final touches on the newly painted porch. "Nobody better say nothin' to me about McKendree bein' a old folks' home."

"What they suppose to call it?" Olivia patted the dirt on top of the last geranium plant to be potted.

"Look around you, girl!" Thumb said, stepping back to take in the complete porch. "McKendree's the Place! The Place to be."

"Thumb," Olivia said, turning her pot to look at it from all sides, "I believe all those paint fumes got to your brain."

Thumb began picking through the bucket of tools. "Could be that I'm the only one with vision," he said. "Smarter than all the rest of y'all put together!"

"Smarter than who?" March set down the empty paint cans he was carrying to the shed. "Who you smarter than, Thumb?"

"Thumb smart?" Georgia came up from the yard to set her two pots of geraniums next to Olivia's. "I must be hearing things."

"Hearing w-what?" Braxton said, joining the group. "I didn't hear anything that m-m-made sense."

Thumb finally found what he had been searching for among the screwdrivers, pliers, and other tools collected in the bucket: the nozzle of the hose. He dug it out and quietly began twisting it onto the end of the long brown hose lying by his feet.

"Y'all a bunch of clowns. All y'all," he said, carefully turning and tightening the nozzle. "Ought to start a carnival. Then y'all could make some money bein' so funny."

None of them noticed Thumb's slight nod, his signal to Tilara, who was standing next to the water faucet at the side of the building. But when water gushed from the hose he held firmly in his hands, they all noticed—and at exactly the same time!

Thumb used the thick spray of water to take command of the lawn and everyone on it. "Y'all *really* funny now!" he yelled. "Maybe now y'all can name yourselves the Wet McKendreeites."

Tilara moved away from the side of the building, laughing at the sight. Happy to have been in on the joke and not one of its victims, she ran to the safety of the porch, where she felt certain Thumb would not turn the hose.

Georgia wrung water from a long clump of her soaked hair. "Thumb can be such a jerk!" she said.

"Aw, com'on, sweet Georgia," March said, sitting beside her on a dry patch of grass Thumb's weapon had missed. "What's a few strings among friends?" he teased, reaching out to smooth her hair.

Georgia jerked her head out of March's reach, sending a fresh spray of water to his face. "Sometimes you as big a fool as he is," she said. Her face pouted, but her voice flirted. "And stop talkin' about me like I got a headful of wet noodles."

Georgia flipped her hair over the top of her head, pulling all of it together to squeeze out the remaining water.

March moved closer to Georgia. "Here," he said, taking the clump of hair in his hands. "Let me help you before somebody starts cookin' up some spaghetti sauce to go with this head."

As she watched March and Georgia from the porch, Tilara pictured her hair's tight tangle when it was wet. Self-consciously, she reached up to pat her hair and breathed a sigh of relief that it had remained dry.

"Okay, T-T-Tilara. You're next!"

Tilara jumped up and steeled herself to receive a spray of water. Then she felt immediately foolish, realizing that the voice could only have come from inside. And never from Thumb.

"Braxton! How did you get in there?"

"I c-came in through the back door t-t-to get away from the water fiend," he said, coming onto the porch and brushing away splatters of water from his face and arms. "So how c-c-come you were in c-cahoots with the minimum m-monster?" he said, smiling.

Laughter bubbled up inside Tilara. "Minimum monster!" she said. "What a good name for Thumb."

"Yeah. Fits him j-just right, in m-my opinion."

They laughed together. It was easy, comfortable. Before thinking about it long enough to stop herself, Tilara reached over to brush away drops of water on Braxton's shoulders.

"Thanks."

Tilara perched on the rail and leaned back against the post. "Thumb's funny. Has he always been like this?"

"More or less." Braxton sat on the edge of the nearby chair. "In Thumb's case, I u-usually think less." Still smiling, he looked into her face. "Don't get me wrong, Thumb's m-my friend and all, but s-sometimes . . ."

"I know what you mean." Tilara grinned. "That's usually the way it is with minimum monsters."

As their carefree laughter floated into the air, Tilara felt satisfaction wrapping all around her.

March watched the two on the porch. While his thoughts questioned, his eyes narrowed. His anger grew and looked for a place to land.

"Hey, Georgia." He began quietly.

"Hmm?" Georgia looked at March over her shoulder.

"How come you never invite Tilara over to your house?"

"What're you talkin' about?"

"Just what I said. How come you never invite her over? You know, like you have Joann and crazy Theodora over to do whatever y'all do when you get together."

"Joann and Theodora are my friends," Georgia

said, pulling her hair together to make one big braid. "Tilara and I aren't ... we just get together here. At McKendree."

"How come you don't like Tilara?"

The sound in his voice made Georgia turn to look into his face. "How you figure that?"

"You know what I mean, Georgia."

"No, I don't. Why don't you tell me?"

March sat up. He pulled at the grass as he talked. "Like that time at Morton's. All of us were trying to be extra friendly to her. After all, we were the only ones there she knew. But you hardly said anything."

"I didn't have to. Like you said, everybody else was makin' her feel right at home."

"There's other things," March went on, rubbing wet blades of grass between his fingers. "You never help out with any of the stuff Tilara does up here. Like the time she wanted somebody to help with the old ladies planting flowers along the walk. You said you'd rather help Thumb paint."

"So?" Georgia's voice was high and tight. "For your information, I hate messin' around in dirt. Why should I volunteer to do something I hate? Why shouldn't I do something I like? And anyhow, I was the one who found the chairs to paint!" Her lip curled up as she spoke.

"See, Georgia, that's exactly what I mean," March said, pushing himself up. "You don't even sound like yourself when you're talkin' about Tilara."

Georgia glared at him. "March, I don't know what on earth you're talking about." She tossed the damp braid over her shoulder.

For a long minute March glared back.

Georgia. She was his friend. Maybe even his best friend. They had shared most of their lives.

The memory of that day under the maple tree began to tug at his thoughts, and the force of his anger melted. He began to feel a strange sadness.

He might already have done something to harm this friendship; he must not do any more. In this thought he reached over to touch Georgia's face.

"Georgia," he began, "I—"

He didn't get a chance to finish. She jerked her head away and got to her feet. "I'm beginning to think McKendree is making you stupid, March Jackson," she hissed. "Maybe that's why you're sitting there, telling me I should be friends with somebody just because I know them, 'cause that's about the stupidest thing I ever heard!"

Angrily she knocked away the last bits of grass from her legs and walked away.

* * *

As the afternoon sun dried all traces of his revenge, Thumb stood again on the walk leading to the porch and waved excitedly to the others. "Hey, y'all. Everybody! Come over here."

Olivia was the first to respond. "What's wrong now, Thumb?"

"Nothin'. Something's right for a change." He motioned for the others to hurry. "In a few minutes Miss Wilson is comin' out to take our picture," he said.

"How come?" March asked.

"Yeah, how c-c-come?" Braxton echoed, coming around the corner with the last of the flowerpots.

"Man, I can't believe y'all." Thumb slapped his forehead, pretending disgust. "Be*cause* we should have a picture of our bee-*u*-tiful new Place. And of our bee-*u*-tiful selves!"

"You know, Thumb's right," March said, moving next to him. "Man, that's an excellent idea."

Thumb beamed. "And I have another idea." He paused, looking around sheepishly. "I think we should give ourselves a name."

"What?" Tilara and Olivia spoke together.

"You already gave us a name, Thumb." Georgia's look was almost a scowl. Seeing that March was looking at her, she smiled coldly. "Remember?

You said we should call ourselves the Real Mc-Kendreeites."

Embarrassed, Thumb began pulling at the belt loops of his shorts. "We need a real name . . . because we're a . . . a real group. Because we come here and . . . and we do stuff together."

He looked down at the walk, waiting, hoping for anyone to say something. "Com'on, y'all. It doesn't have to be fancy—" he said, finally looking at the others.

"Something like the McKendreeite Kids, maybe?" Tilara said, wanting to giggle but jumping in to give him support.

"Don't laugh," Thumb said, glad for any kind of response. "That's not so bad. Well, maybe not Mc-Kendreeites. You know, we were kind of makin' fun of Miss Wilson when we called ourselves that. But Miss Wilson, she ain't so bad. She's okay. Maybe just the McKendree Kids wouldn't be so bad."

Olivia started shaking her head. "Thumb, maybe you'd better stick with one idea at a time. This name business is—"

Just at that moment Miss Wilson burst through the door, camera in hand.

"Okay, McKendree Crowd," she said in her usual take-charge way. "Arrange yourselves on this lovely

156

porch you've created so I can record the occasion for posterity."

After a few minutes the portrait was in place. Braxton and March stood on the top step. Georgia and Tilara stood on the second step down, and Thumb and Olivia on the third.

Views of the porch they had renovated were on either side of them. The repaired railings had been painted a sparkling white, along with the wicker chairs and swing with its new chain. All were stuffed with cushions in rainbow shades of blue and green. Lined with pots of geraniums, the newly sanded porch floor gleamed with fresh varnish.

"Ready?" Miss Wilson said, the camera in front of her face.

"Ready, Miss Wilson," Thumb called out just before the shutter clicked on the six smiling faces. "The MCs are ready!"

Georgia

Georgia knew from her nana's end of the conversation who had telephoned. After running to the upstairs extension, she jerked the receiver from its cradle and pressed it close to her ear. "Hello? Mother?"

Knowing her granddaughter had picked up, Loretta Callaway hung up. Continuing to fold the fresh sheets and towels, she listened to snatches of Georgia's conversation.

"Mother, when are you coming?"

Loretta Callaway could imagine her daughter Esther's soft sigh at the other end. It would be the same sigh she had heard a few moments earlier when she had asked the same question.

"Why not? You always come in the summer. Always."

The music that had been in Georgia's voice when she picked up the phone faded. She had heard the same thing Loretta had been told. That things were very busy in Chicago. It wouldn't be wise to leave for a vacation anytime soon.

"Then couldn't I come to Chicago to visit you this time?"

Mrs. Callaway gripped the ends of the pillowcase she was folding. Her breath locked in her chest as she wondered what the response to this question would be.

"But I wouldn't mind staying in your apartment while you went to work. Really I wouldn't. I could shop for groceries and fix dinner and—"

Georgia promising things she never did at home. Hearing this, Loretta Callaway almost smiled.

"But there's nothing at McKendree I'd miss."

Georgia's voice was getting flatter.

"Yeah, I know I said we're helping out. But it wouldn't matter if I wasn't there. It would be okay if I never went back to McKendree."

The anger was a new, added tone in Georgia's voice.

"Yeah, March goes, too, but so what? It doesn't mean—"

All the linens were now folded and stacked. There was no reason for Mrs. Callaway to keep standing there.

"But why, Mother? Why won't you ever let me come visit you?"

Hearing this, Loretta Callaway rushed to pick up her basket and get back to the kitchen. Although she was sure it would not be given in a careless moment over the telephone, she still hurried from the answer she knew must someday come. In this knowledge her heart went out to the two on the phone: Georgia, her youngest grandbaby, and Esther, her favorite child.

Esther. The practically new bride whose husband had been killed in the mines when their daughter was still an infant. A woman whose pain and sadness had reached so deep, she took back her family name of Callaway as one way to forget. Then, turning away from her baby, the family who loved her, and the town in which she had grown up, fallen in love, and gotten married, Esther had moved to the big city, leaving all of her past life behind.

Esther. Georgia's mother, who now passed for white.

17

Maggie Wilson looked out at the group gathered on the porch: the MCs—as Thumb said they had named themselves—and Mr. Reese, Miss Alpha, Mr. Craighead, and Cloelle. Mr. Reese's story had everyone's attention, even though most had to strain to hear the crackly voice.

"I don't know which pleases me more," she said, "the sound of Mr. Reese's voice or the laughter of those young people."

Standing behind Miss Wilson, Dr. P. surveyed the scene over her shoulder. "Thankfully this summer has brought us a heavy dose of both," he said.

The two stood quietly, guessing the other's thoughts about Mr. Reese, whose frailness had increased over the past winter. Who sometimes hadn't been expected to enjoy the joy of another summer.

"According to what I heard when I was out on the porch earlier," Dr. P. said, "today's saga is taking the kids all the way back to the plantation."

Miss Wilson shook her head and laughed. "Gracious me. Reese has lived through a bunch of stuff, but he's not *that* old."

Dr. P. kept his voice low. "He has some firsthand plantation stories, though. Well, almost firsthand. He used to hear them from his father, who was born into slavery."

Remaining behind the screen door, they listened as the telling time continued.

"Your grandfather w-w-worked in the house?" Braxton was sitting on a stool beside Mr. Reese.

"Lord, no." The crackly voice chuckled. "My granddaddy was too black to work in the big house. They liked to keep the light skins as house slaves."

"See there, Braxton?" Thumb said from his spot next to the railing. "You'd been outta luck on the plantation. Stuck out in the fields doin' hard labor."

"What makes you think *any* of it *w-w-wasn't* h-hard labor?" Braxton's dark eyes flashed. "At least b-b-black was an honorable color."

"What are you talkin' about, man?" Thumb's eyes narrowed.

"Think about it, Thumb," Olivia said, her voice flying and her words commanding. "Think about all the African women on the plantation that were . . . were . . ."

"Dishonored," Cloelle offered, patting Olivia on her shoulder.

"Yeah, dishonored." Olivia smiled at Cloelle. "Thanks, Miz Haynes," she said. "And then think about the results," she added, looking at Thumb.

"Let Mr. Reese g-go on, y'all." Braxton moved his stool closer to the old man.

"It's goin', it's goin'," Mr. Reese said, quickening the rocking motion of his chair. "All this stuff you young'uns are talkin' about is part of the story."

Soon afterward, Mr. Reese wound up his story. The group began to break up.

"It's simply amazing how you remember all those things, Reese," Mr. Craighead said, getting up. "You're a walking history book."

"Indeed so," Cloelle said. She looked at Tilara and the others. "All of you should take advantage of that," she added. "There are very few history books in your classrooms with the information Mr. Reese is giving you."

Everyone but Braxton followed Cloelle and the director into the building. Braxton remained on the stool near Mr. Reese's feet.

"Miss Haynes s-sounds like my father," he said, looking into the old weathered face.

"How's that?" Mr. Reese asked.

"When we s-started coming up here, he said that sp-p-p-pending time with folks who've lived history would be a good idea." Braxton smiled. "N-now I know what he meant."

Mr. Reese looked down at Braxton. His eyes twinkled. "I don't think spending time with us old folks is the only good idea you've found at McKendree, young fella," he said.

"What do you mean?" Braxton moved to the railing across from Mr. Reese's chair and leaned back.

"What I mean is, I seen you looking at young Miss Georgia." Mr. Reese's grin showed the dark spaces in his mouth where teeth had been missing for years. "I've seen you looking, and I know what you been thinking." He rubbed the lower part of his left arm, a gesture that lately seemed to relax him. "I know because I can remember feeling the same way when I was a young pup, just a mite older than you."

Mr. Reese rested his head against the back of the chair. "I can remember clear as anything wanting to have a fine, high-toned girl like Miss Georgia on my arm."

Braxton looked down at the porch floor, not trusting himself to say anything. The sounds of the birds skipped across the silence.

"Yep, I remember that well," Mr. Reese said, gazing into the distance beyond the porch. "I wanted that same kind of girl for myself. The same kind of girl the white boys had. The kind of girl white boys been sayin' is the most beautiful in the world. They was even sayin' that to us by the kind of gals they picked to be in the house with them down on the plantation!"

Mr. Reese cackled. It was a familiar sound that often punctuated his conversation. "A girl with skin like a smooth yellow peach and long straight hair down her back." Mr. Reese looked at Braxton and winked. "A girl like that Georgia."

"You think I like Georgia 'cause of the w-way sh-she looks?" Braxton shoved his hands in his pockets as he determined to make his feelings clear. "Mr. Reese, Georgia's n-nice. Sh-she's real nice. She can't help being l-l-l-light skinned. It's the way sh-she was born!"

Mr. Reese's laugh was loud and full. "Don't think I ever heard it defended quite like that before, Braxton," he said. "But I guess you're right. I guess Miss high-toned Georgia can't no more help being that way than you young colored boys can help thinking that's the best way for a girl to be."

Mr. Reese shook his head. "I figure it must go all the way back to being on that d——, that plantation, where they actually tried to make us believe it was better to be a slave in the house 'stead of one out in the fields." He snorted. "I guess we got a few more generations still to go 'fore we'll know for certain there ain't no difference!"

"Am I missing another story?" Tilara poked her head around the screen door.

"We w-w-were just talkin'," Braxton answered quickly. Tilara's voice startled him. And embarrassed him, although he wasn't certain why.

Tilara came out onto the porch and walked over to Mr. Reese. "Can I bring you anything?" she asked. "Would you like a sweater? It's getting cooler."

"I'm fine, Miss Tilara. Just fine. The air feels good on these tired bones," Mr. Reese said, rubbing his arm.

"Braxton, are you getting ready to do something? I mean, we want you to come in for a minute if you aren't busy." Tilara's voice was quiet.

"Okay," Braxton said. "Wh-what's up?"

"We're planning a birthday party," she said. "A surprise party for Miss Alpha. For next Thursday."

"Won't Alpha love that!" Mr. Reese cackled with pleasure.

"Ummm," Tilara said, nodding her head. "It was Georgia's idea." Her voice brightened as she looked at Mr. Reese. "You won't let on, will you, Mr. Reese?" she asked, knowing as they all did how the old man liked to tease his friend.

"Shucks, no!" Mr. Reese settled back in his chair. "Then I wouldn't have the pleasure of seeing her drop her teeth when everybody yells, 'Surprise!' "

"Why d-don't you come help with the plans?" Braxton moved beside Mr. Reese's chair, ready to help the old gentleman up and support him as he walked.

"Lord, no," Mr. Reese said emphatically. "One of the great pleasures of age is doing none of the work and havin' all the fun."

"It's getting cold, Mr. Reese," Tilara said again.

"I'll be fine, little lady. Just fine," Mr. Reese said. "You two run along. And make sure you cook up something to surprise that old bird good!"

After Tilara and Braxton went inside, Mr. Reese rocked in the cooling air, imagining the pleasure of his old friend when next Thursday rolled around. The pleasure of the entire place. "A surprise party brings something good to everybody."

Resting back, he began thinking about the young people inside planning still something else. Youngsters who had come to McKendree and been like a summer blessing of gold. Especially Braxton, who had found a special place in his heart.

"Braxton." He whispered the name into the soft wind blowing from the river. "How I'd like to be around to see what you turn out to be."

He closed his eyes, looking into his mind as if into a mirror of the future. "You got good character, boy," he said to the image clear only to him. "But right now that character ought to help you see how Tilara's eyes look after you the same way your eyes look after that Georgia girl!"

The sound of Mr. Reese's satisfied cackle lifted into the wind. Hearing it in the great room, the MCs smiled as they huddled together to make their plans for the party.

18

Dr. Adolphus Courtland stopped at the doorway of the great room, delighting in the sight before him.

They were gathered around the large, round table in the middle of the room. March stood next to Tilara, his face a golden profile against the deep chocolate of her cheeks and hair. On Tilara's other side, Olivia's freckled, sugarcane face peeked from under a crown of reddish curls as she leaned close to Thumb, whose face and hair matched the color of shaded desert sand. Next to him, Georgia's sun-daisy face was framed by the yellow-brown ribbon curls that fell across her cheeks and shoulder. Completing the circle was Braxton, his ebony face and hair rising above the others. A head of the first kings on earth.

Dr. P. whispered lines from one of his favorite poems:

> "The night is beautiful,
> So the faces of my people . . . "

Then, locking the picture inside himself, he strolled over to the table.

"So, whachu think?" Thumb was saying, biting on his lip at the needy sound of his words.

Olivia was the first to answer. "Thumb, it's good! It's really good!"

" 'G-good' doesn't d-do it justice, Livvy," Braxton said, bending closer to the picture. "It's b-better than good. It's f-fantastic."

Hardly able to believe that Braxton had paid him a compliment, Thumb was momentarily speechless.

Looking over Braxton's shoulder, Dr. P. saw the object of their attention: a painting spread across the table. "It's the chorus line from the old Cotton Club," he said, appreciation clear in his voice.

"You knew what it was right away, didn't you, Dr. P.?" Thumb said, again reaching out for approval.

"One glance was all it took." Dr. P. smiled at Thumb. "Anybody who knows about that line at the Cotton Club will recognize this right away."

Thumb beamed.

Dr. P. studied the painting. "I realize that Alpha talks endlessly about her life at the Cotton Club, but I never knew her descriptions were so detailed."

"Yeah, she goes on about that place," Thumb said, "but I did this from a picture." He carefully pulled a worn photograph from an envelope. It showed a row of young, light-skinned women. All were dressed in short dresses, close-fitting hats, and white tap shoes with bows. His painting matched the image almost exactly.

Thumb handed the photo to Dr. P. "Miss Alpha's been asking me to draw something for her ever since she saw that picture I made to show what the porch was gonna look like," he said, losing the struggle to hold back his grin. "Tilara saw this photograph in that scrapbook Miss Alpha's always showing around and said it seemed like the perfect picture to paint."

Georgia tossed her head, shaking the curls back across her shoulders. "Thumb was going to give the picture to Miss Alpha at the end of the summer, but I convinced him to finish it in time for her birthday," she said, cutting her eyes in Tilara's direction. "And now that we're planning a surprise party, this'll be a wonderful gift for Miss Alpha, don't you think, Dr. P.?"

Dr. P. nodded his head, anticipating the reaction of the woman he had known for years. "She'll be thrilled. Simply thrilled."

The praise continued. Only Tilara remained silent, her thoughts hidden behind a small smile and lowered eyes.

Olivia trailed her finger along the edges of the picture as she stared at it. "You know something, y'all? Miss Alpha, well, she still look kind of like this."

March laughed. "Livvy, you must think Miss Alpha's gonna put you in her will," he said. "She can only *wish* she looked this young."

Georgia tossed her curls again, this time in March's direction. "You not being fair, March," she said. "Miss Alpha doesn't look all that old."

Dr. Courtland chuckled as he pulled a handkerchief from his back pocket. "That's because she's not all *that* old, as you put it."

"Then how come she's here?" Olivia blurted and then stopped herself, not wanting to sound rude. "You know what I mean, Dr. P., this a old folks' home, right? And Miss Alpha, well, she gotta be a little old . . ." Her voice trailed off as she watched Dr. P. carefully remove his glasses.

"Don't misunderstand me, Livvy," he said. "Alpha isn't young. And she's definitely older than she looks. Matter of fact, she was one of the oldest of the Cotton Club dancers. . . ."

As he continued, Tilara focused on the fluttering of the handkerchief he used to clean his glasses, wanting the movement to pull her mind away from the details about Miss Alpha that seemed to go on and on.

Lost her job in New York . . . had difficulty building a lasting economic foundation . . . confined to a wheelchair . . . no family to speak of . . . no place else to go . . .

"That does it. I'm definitely staying young forever."

The unexpected whisper in her ear startled Tilara. "What?" she said. Turning her head, she found herself looking directly into the amber centers of March's eyes.

"Never gonna get old," he said. "That's the thing to do, don't you think?" His grin widened as his eyes narrowed.

"I guess," she said, looking down at the uneven surfaces of the wood floor.

The group was breaking apart. Georgia called out to remind everyone about other preparations needed for the party. "We got a lot to do, y'all. Everybody needs to help."

Olivia and I are supposed to help with the cake. . . .

"Excuse me," Tilara said to March, feeling the need to say something and unable to think of anything else. Then, keeping her eyes on the floor, she crossed in front of him and walked in Olivia's direction.

Through his half-closed eyes, March watched Tilara's beige skirt ripple as she moved across the floor. Smiling to himself, he decided it was okay that nothing more had been said. Thursday would be a time to say more. Miss Alpha's birthday party was planned for Thursday. A party would be the perfect setting for talking to Tilara. He'd say everything he wanted to then.

The hand on his shoulder tore March away from his thoughts. "Hey, man," Thumb asked, "you still gonna help me frame this picture like you said?"

"You know you can count on me, my man," March said, throwing his arm around Thumb's shoulder. "Let's get started now. We gotta make sure everything for this party will be perfect!"

19

As she had done countless times already, Tilara popped open the blue-and-gold tin and inhaled the delightful contents: cinnamon-studded orange halves, bay leaves, cloves, and dried apples and berries. Then she ran her finger along the soft length of velvet ribbon, anxious to see it wrapped around the box but strangely reluctant to put it in place.

"It'll make a wonderful gift," Cloelle had said, showing Tilara the special mixture she used to freshen her closets and cabinets. "You can put it in one of those cookie tins I keep in the pantry."

Tilara had lined the inside of the tin with rose-colored tissue before adding generous scoops of Cloelle's mixture. The only thing left to do was snap the lid shut and secure it with the ribbon. Then it would be the gift it was intended to be. A birthday gift for Miss Alpha.

Do I want to give her this?

The question had nagged Tilara all morning, especially since the plan was to make Thumb's painting a gift from all of them. It was what Thumb said he wanted.

Why am I giving her something else?

Tilara stared into the spicy mixture nestled in the rose paper like the lush center of an exotic flower and began collecting the images she had of Miss Alpha.

Miss Alpha, who had been the first McKendree resident she had spoken to. The elderly woman's "Hi, darlin', I'm so happy to see you" had made her feel welcomed.

Since that first day, however, she often caught Miss Alpha staring at her. As if there were something about Tilara that wasn't exactly the way it was supposed to be. Whatever the something was always made Miss Alpha smile weakly and then look away whenever Tilara met her eyes.

Miss Alpha, who was happiest when Georgia was around. "Where's my girl today?" she whined to Dr. P. the day Georgia had to stay in Warren Springs and go somewhere with her grandmother. "I don't want you coming up here without my girl, Doctor."

So let Georgia give her something special.

Tilara dipped her hand delicately into the tin, liking the crunchy feel of the dried herbs and fruit. She moved her fingers through it, causing a few of the pieces to spill onto the table.

"You can always take a minute to do something nice for someone, Tilara. It makes them feel special, and you'll feel good about it, too."

Her father's words fell across her like a heavy blanket. Words designed to control what she should do and how she should think about things. Even how she should feel.

Tilara dug deeper into the mixture. More pieces spilled out as another image of Miss Alpha drifted across her mind.

Miss Alpha sitting with March. Listening to his phony compliments and looking at him with fluttering eyelashes. Talking to him from behind her hand, which she had placed next to her mouth as if her fingers were the ribs of a fan. Saying, "When a girl loses her looks, she doesn't have anything left, you know. We've got to hold on to our looks as long as we can."

"Anybody who thinks like that doesn't deserve a special gift. Certainly not from me!"

Tilara's words spilled out along with still more of the spicy mixture. Big and little pieces of it now littered the table. Tilara stared at the mess.

"Well, Miss Alpha, darlin'," she said to herself, "the fact is, seeing the mess on this table, I wouldn't dream of giving it to you. Especially knowing how you feel about the way things look."

Tilara began picking at the pieces, flicking them around on the table. "As a matter of fact, anybody who thinks that looks are the most important thing in the world doesn't really deserve any kind of gift from me!"

Suddenly, without any reason she could think of, Tilara began to giggle. After a long moment she started putting things back together. Gathering the scattered bits, she repacked the tissue and then carefully pulled together its edges and removed everything from the tin.

She held up the fragrant bundle in front of her and turned it around to look at it from all sides. "Hmm," she said, wondering aloud. Then she picked up the ribbon and carefully looped it around the base of the gathered part. She finished by tying a neat bow.

Again she held up the bundle in front of her. "I think Miss Bertha will love this. It'll remind her of her kitchen." She set it carefully on the table and picked up the tin. "I'll give her this, too—*after* I fill it with some delicious ginger cookies."

Moving across the kitchen, Tilara placed the tin on the counter by the sink, reached for the cookbook on the shelf above the counter, and turned to a familiar page.

Ginger cookies.

Getting the apron from its hook, she remembered one more thing she wanted to do before gathering the ingredients.

The record was at the top of the stack by the Victrola. They had bought it only two days earlier. Cloelle promised that Tilara could take it with her when she left.

In seconds the record was on the turntable and music began pouring through the small valley home. Within minutes Tilara had begun sifting flour and measuring spices into the heavy yellow-and-brown mixing bowl that had belonged to her grandmother.

With her foot tapping and hands moving confidently, she began to sing. "I'm gonna moo-ove on up a little higher . . ."

20

 "Shh."

Georgia poked her head in the space between the sliding doors that opened onto the great room. "Shhh," she said again, this time louder. "Dr. P. is bringing her down the hallway now."

March and Braxton stood ready to push the doors open. Tilara, Olivia, and Thumb hurried to light the last few candles on the huge cake. The flickering circle would be the first thing Miss Alpha saw when they pushed her wheelchair into the room.

"Miss Alpha! You look so pretty today." Georgia's voice echoed in the long hallway. It was the signal they had been waiting for.

"Why, thank you, darlin'. This old dress is one of—"

The rest of Miss Alpha's words were lost. Right on cue, the doors were pushed open, and the entire room erupted with "Happy birthday!"

"Good gracious! What is all of this?" Miss Alpha's surprised voice squeaked above the chorus of singing and well wishes that followed her across the room.

Dr. P. and Georgia rolled her over to the cake

now ablaze with candles. Tilara was the last to join the group gathered by the cake to help Miss Alpha blow out her candles. She had watched the grand entrance standing alongside Miss Bertha.

Mr. Reese came close to the wheelchair to take the hand of his friend. "What you got to say about this, old girl? We fooled you good, and don't you make out like we didn't," he cackled.

"I should say so! Why, I never suspected a thing. Not once!" Miss Alpha beamed, enjoying both the surprise and the attention. Her amber eyes were bright in a face the color of cream kissed by a drop of coffee.

"Go on, Alpha," Mrs. Richardson called out from her chair by the window. "You know you suspected something. That's why you put on that red dress. It's your favorite."

"Yes, Alpha. I saw you snooping around the other day," Mr. Jeffries said from his spot on the couch.

"Why, I was doing no such thing!" Miss Alpha pushed at the armrests of her chair. "And I put this dress on because—"

"Because she looks beautiful in it," Cloelle interrupted, "and every woman wants to look especially beautiful on her birthday." Cloelle moved next to Miss Alpha's chair and put her hands gently on the woman's shoulders.

"Why, thank you, darlin'," Miss Alpha cooed to Cloelle.

"You do look pretty, Miss Alpha." Georgia leaned over to kiss her cheek.

"Com'on, Braxton. Let's see what you can do on that gee-tar!" March said. He was anxious to steer the party in the direction he had carefully plotted in his mind. "Let's hear some dancin' music."

Braxton had brought his guitar, planning to strum "Happy Birthday" at the critical moment. That opportunity had passed, and the guitar still rested in its case.

"I don't play d-dancin' music, man," Braxton said. "I d-dance myself to that music."

"Then let's get some music on for dancin'!" March said.

Going to Miss Bertha's Victrola, which they had borrowed from the kitchen, March put on one of the records belonging to his father he had brought with him. Soon the harmonies of "Mood Indigo" filled the room.

As if following a script he had outlined for the evening, March first snapped off the bright overhead light, welcoming in the soft glow of twilight.

Next, he walked over to Georgia. "May I have this dance?" he requested, bowing with a flourish.

Hoping to conceal the pleasure dancing in her heart, Georgia shrugged with indifference and stepped without a word into March's waiting arms.

A space for dancing had been cleared beside the old piano next to the windows. March moved easily within the space, gracefully leading Georgia to the rhythms. They made a lovely picture that all the others watched.

It was working out as March had hoped: He had everyone's attention and was showing how good he was. He would ask Tilara next.

Halfway through the song, Olivia took Thumb by the hand and led him onto the floor. Then, surprising everyone, Mr. Jeffries extended both of his hands, one to Mrs. Richardson and the other to Miss Coleman, who rarely left her room and had been happily welcomed to the festivities.

"At our age, being a threesome is better than being a couple," Mr. Jeffries said, holding the hands of both women and guiding them in making their own small circle.

Laughing and wanting to join in, Braxton held out his hand to Tilara.

* * *

183

Feeling his arms around her and the gentleness of his touch, Tilara held her breath.

I wish this could last forever.

"Y-you're a good dancer, Tilara."

Tilara smiled her thanks, not thinking that being so close to her cheek, Braxton couldn't see her face.

They moved easily across the floor. Tilara wanted to close her eyes. To feel that she and Braxton were the only ones moving through the cloud of sound. But then the record ended and the mood was over.

"Hold on, March." Thumb's excited voice drew everyone's attention. "We got somethin' to do before you put on another record."

March's eyes were no more than slits when he threw his glance to Thumb. "What are you talkin' about, man?" he asked, struggling to keep his voice even.

"You know," Thumb whispered, moving close to March. "The picture. Miss Alpha's present."

"Oh, yeah. The picture." March forced his lips to make a smile.

Thumb turned on the bright overhead light and reached for the wrapped package behind the door.

Miss Alpha clasped her hands together as she looked at the painting Thumb held in front of her. "Why, it's beautiful, Thumb. Just beautiful!" Her smile embraced the entire room.

"That's . . . There we are! Me and all the others. At the Cotton Club, just like we used to be!" Miss Alpha's voice got higher with each exclamation. "How on earth did you do it?"

"I snuck out your picture." Thumb spoke through a smile almost as big as Miss Alpha's. "You know, the one you showed us one time when you were telling us about how you used to dance there."

"Yes, I did, didn't I?" Miss Alpha breathed, touching the picture gently. "And you made a picture even more wonderful than my photograph."

"I painted it, but the gift is from all of us, Miss Alpha," Thumb said, pointing to the double-line signature that read "Horace T. Martin and the MCs."

Miss Alpha opened her arms to Thumb. "But you did it. Come over here, young man, and let Miss Alpha give you some sugar."

Bending to receive Miss Alpha's hug and kiss, Thumb saw March's face over her shoulder. His eyes pleaded with March not to snicker.

"I will cherish this always," Miss Alpha said. "And I will cherish *you* always because of it."

Thumb walked around the room with the painting

to help the other McKendreeites get a better look. Words of praise followed him. March watched impatiently, wanting things to move forward in the direction he'd planned and deciding that in the meantime it would be a good time to get a breath of fresh air.

Back in front of Miss Alpha and full of new confidence, Thumb decided the time was right for getting an answer to a curious question.

"Miss Alpha, why does Mr. Reese call you Brown Skin? You aren't really, and from that photograph you never was."

Miss Alpha laughed and tossed her head. A thin, silky curl fell across her forehead. "Why, you can't tell it from that old photo—it's faded quite a bit, you know—but in that chorus line I *was* the brown-skinned one."

She lowered her voice and moved her head closer to Thumb. "I was lucky even to be hired, you know. Why, in those days girls any browner than me couldn't even get a chance to try out for the line, no matter how good they were at hoofing."

Miss Alpha turned to look Georgia's direction. "Georgia, honey," she said, "don't you remember me tellin' you the other day how much you reminded me of Effie Harper, that friend of mine?"

Without waiting for an answer, Miss Alpha

turned back to look at Thumb. "Effie was Georgia's color. Most of the girls were. And a prettier bunch of women you never saw."

Miss Alpha laughed. "In that crowd I *was* the dark one. Not so brown to not be pretty, mind you, but darker nevertheless." She tossed her head grandly. "Reese started calling me Brown Skin to tease me."

An uncomfortable quiet drifted across the room. Georgia walked to the back of Miss Alpha's chair, taking special care not to look at anyone in particular. "Miss Alpha," she said, "are you ready for more punch?"

"Did I ever tell you how Reese and I met while I was working at the Cotton Club?" Miss Alpha's chatter continued as Georgia pushed the wheelchair toward the punch bowl and cups. "Why, that's quite a story. . . ."

Tilara found herself standing beside Thumb as the two of them watched the backs of Georgia and Miss Alpha.

"Miss Alpha must be getting——" Thumb began.

"Thumb, what are you going to do with the painting?" Interrupting him, Tilara's voice was higher and louder than usual. She pointed to the framed canvas still in his hands.

187

Thumb looked down. He hadn't realized he was still holding the painting. "Think I should take it to Miss Alpha's room?"

"Yes, that's a good idea. Do you need help?"

"No, I can manage." Thumb tilted his head in the direction of the opened sliding doors. "See, no doors to open."

Tilara looked around the room. "Do you know where, uh, Braxton and the others went?"

"Braxton's probably somewhere talking with Mr. Reese like he usually is." Thumb hoisted the painting to hold it more securely. "Olivia went with Miss Bertha to get something from the kitchen, and I don't know where March went."

"I think I'll go look for them. I'll see you later. Before you leave. You know, to go home."

Without waiting for any response from Thumb and looking neither left nor right, Tilara walked from the great room into the hallway. Her eyes found and rested on the doorway at the end of the hall that led to the safe blackness of the approaching night.

21

Tilara rushed down the corridor, her thoughts racing as swiftly as her feet.

Stupid, stupid old woman.

A cold rush of memory crowded another picture into her mind: the face of Mrs. Henry.

Mrs. Henry. The teacher whose brainwashed mind spewed a special brand of poison. A person who had been taught to hate her own dark skin and who year after year infested her students with that same hatred.

Miss Alpha's just like old lady Henry—stupider than sin.

The thoughts beat like drums in Tilara's ears. They pounded out each step she took. Finally reaching the worn screen door, she placed her hands on its edges and was about to push it open when she heard the familiar cackle. It was coming from the porch. She stopped in the darkened doorway and stood without moving.

"Aw, com'on, Mr. Reese. You making that up."

March. The only person who would dare tell Mr. Reese he's not telling the truth.

Holding in her breath along with her thoughts, Tilara waited for the other voices. For Braxton, who she knew would put March in his place.

But there were no other voices. Only March and Mr. Reese were on the porch.

Tilara looked behind her, down the hallway she had just walked along. The bright light from the great room fell like a square in the center of the corridor. The other lights were ribbons of yellow and white along the edges of closed doors lining both of its sides.

She turned around and retraced her steps, staying within the shadows as she passed the entrance to the great room.

Mustn't interrupt Queen Alpha. She might be in the middle of one of her stories. Why, that just wouldn't do.

The fury of Tilara's thoughts made it difficult for her to breathe normally. When she reached the office door, she stood against the wall and took several deep breaths. They calmed her as a plea rang in her head.

Please be in the office, Aunt Cloelle. Please be there and ready to go home. Please.

"Aunt Cloelle?" Tilara called softly, gently tapping the door with one hand and turning the T-shaped door handle with the other.

She walked into the dimly lit room. "Aunt Cloelle?" she called again.

A single lamp burned on her aunt's desk, but the office was empty. Tilara walked over to the desk to turn off the light and saw Miss Alpha's picture on top of a pile of papers. It was the photograph Thumb had copied. She picked up the photograph and stared at it.

A line of women stared at Tilara from the photo. Twelve women dressed exactly alike, each one with her right leg kicked out. Twelve women, each with light skin.

Tilara tossed the picture back on the desk, turned off the desk light, and started to the door. Just as she reached for the handle, the door pushed toward her from the other side. It was Thumb. Unaware that anyone else was there, he walked right into her.

"Hey!" Thumb fell backward against the door-frame.

"Thumb, it's me. Tilara." Tilara reached for the switch on the wall by the door. The ceiling light washed over the room.

"Tilara! You scared the mess outta me!"

"Sorry. I didn't realize anyone was coming through the door."

"Yeah, and I couldn't see nobody in the room."

"Of course you couldn't. I disappear in the dark." Tilara had clamped her teeth together to catch the words before they were out of her mouth. But they slipped through.

"Aw, com'on, Tilara. You know that's not what I meant."

Thumb came into the room. He was carrying the painting. "Miss Cloelle told me to put the painting in here. She's going to hang it in Miss Alpha's room tomorrow."

He spotted the photograph Tilara had tossed on the desk. "Whew," he said, his voice showing relief. "I thought I was gonna have to hunt for that thing. I couldn't remember where I put it, and I told Miss Cloelle I'd get it for her."

"How come she wants it?" Tilara asked

"She gonna get a frame for it. She said that'll be her birthday present for Miss Alpha."

Thumb picked up the photograph. "Miss Alpha sure does love this picture," he said, looking at it. "You know what she said this group was called?"

"I can't imagine." The words were coated with sarcasm and tumbled out before Tilara could stop them.

Thumb didn't appear to notice. "The Hot Chocolates," he said, putting heavy emphasis on the last word. "Can you beat that? A name like Chocolate for this group of skinny marshmallows."

Tilara's laugh was forced. Even so, she noticed a look of relief on Thumb's face as the two of them laughed together.

"That's old-timey stuff Miss Alpha talks about," Thumb said, reaching for the painting he had left by the door. "Nobody looks at people's color. Nobody with good sense, anyhow."

Thumb kept talking while he carried the painting to a space on the opposite side of the room. "Only a fool would think a girl is pretty just 'cause she's light skinned."

He moved aside the pile of books on the floor to make room for the painting. "Sometimes I wonder about Braxton. He thinks Georgia is fine as wine."

Thumb carefully propped the frame against the wall in the space he had cleared. "Don't get me wrong. Georgia and me, we're friends, and she *is* fine. But a lot of guys are hung up on her color. And if you ask me, Braxton's one of them."

Thumb stepped back to look at where he had placed the painting. Checking to make certain he had chosen a good spot. "Yeah, sometimes I catch

Braxton lookin' at Georgia when he can't see me watchin' him, and ..."

Satisfied that his work of art would be safe, Thumb turned around to look at Tilara while he finished his sentence. "... and he's lookin' at her like ... "

His voice trailed away. He was talking to an empty room. Tilara was no longer there. The door was halfway open, and she was gone.

Tilara could still hear Thumb's voice as she rushed again down the corridor.

Sometimes I catch Braxton lookin' at Georgia ...

She wanted to close her eyes, thinking that this might shut out the voice repeating the same thing, over and over.

Sometimes I catch Braxton lookin' at Georgia ...

The realization pounded its way to the front of Tilara's mind. Braxton and Georgia. Braxton usually ending up where Georgia was. Braxton laughing first at Georgia's little jokes. Braxton. The first to volunteer when Georgia asked for help, and the last to stay behind.

Sometimes I catch Braxton lookin' at Georgia ...

"Makin' him just as stupid as ..."

Tilara's angry thoughts rushed out of her mouth in a growling whisper. The sound surprised her own ears and stopped her in her tracks.

She was standing in the middle of the square of light sent from the great room. She looked in. Except for Mrs. Marshall and Mrs. Hopson sitting at a table, playing double solitaire, it was empty.

Still standing in the doorway, Tilara looked to her left, the direction from which she had come. The back entrance to the building was just beyond her aunt's office. She looked to the right, the direction of the front entrance just ahead.

That's probably where everyone is. Mr. Reese, March, Olivia. Probably Georgia. And Braxton.

The burning in her stomach spread into her chest.

Braxton, you're a whole lot stupider than I ever thought!

Pivoting on her heel and holding her head high, she turned right and headed to the porch.

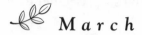 # March

March made his way back up the path with the camera he had gone to Dr. P.'s car to get. He had brought it to record the event for Miss Alpha but had forgotten it in the earlier excitement.

The excitement had faded. Completely. There would definitely be no more dancing. Cardplaying regulars had turned off the radio and turned on all the lights. The old folks had taken back their room. Might as well take the pictures Dr. P. had suggested. Nothing better left to do.

Standing on the steps of the porch with the starless night sky at his back, March wondered if his flash and the dim porch light would provide enough light. He held up the camera, positioned the viewfinder in front of his eye, and moved the lens along the scene to check it out.

Miss Alpha's wheelchair had been rolled next to the rocking chair where Mr. Reese sat. Georgia stood behind Miss Alpha, talking to Braxton, who leaned against the building.

A cooing sound caught his attention.

"Why, Reese, shame on you, talkin' all that trash." Miss Alpha. The laugh that followed was almost the giggle of a girl.

Both Miss Alpha and Mr. Reese were within a yellow triangle of porch light. Sitting close to each other. Very close.

Behind the frame of the camera's lens, March saw Mr. Reese's thin, long fingers gently stroke Miss Alpha's left hand and the sparkle of her rings as she raised her right hand to her face. The move of a young girl flirting.

March leaned in closer. He watched Mr. Reese lift the fragile hand and then bend slowly to touch it with his lips.

"Well, looka here. He loves her! Old man Reese loves himself some Miss Alpha. Get out!" March spoke softly to himself. Then he lowered his camera as if making sure the picture hadn't imagined itself inside the rectangle box.

It hadn't. Everything was clear. Right there within the splash of yellowish light, Mr. Reese was loving Miss Alpha with his eyes and a gentle kiss.

At that moment Tilara entered the scene. Softly opening the door, she stepped onto the porch.

Behind the safety of his camera, March stared, and whispered to himself, "At the next party I'll kiss you just like old man Reese is—"

Then it hit him. "A party. That's what's making old man Reese so bold! A party makes gettin' close easy."

Realizing that his mutterings were getting loud, March turned quickly toward the night. But the plan continued to form in his mind. "That's what we'll do. The MCs will have a party. A party for us! It'll be a perfect way to get close to Tilara. Perfect!"

Turning back to the scene, March lifted the camera again to his face. "Okay, folks, get ready to smile pretty," he called. "All together, now, say, 'Parteeeeee!' "

22

"We gonna party!" Thumb strutted across the porch, snapping his fingers. "Like March said, it's time for us to do something nice for *us*, and we gonna party hard!"

"Thumb, sit down and shut up." Olivia pulled at Thumb's sweater. "Be quiet so we can make some plans."

"Yeah, Thumb," Braxton agreed. "We know we w-want to have a party. What we need from you are s-suggestions."

"So, who's s-s-s-stopping you from making one?" Thumb hissed back at Braxton.

Tilara leaned against the railing next to the steps, taking everything in and saying nothing.

"Okay, first thing we need to do is pick a date." March took center stage. "It should be a Friday . . . no, it should be a Saturday night. What do you think?"

"Sounds good to me," Thumb said. Braxton and Olivia nodded their heads in agreement. Georgia shrugged her shoulders in a "fine with me" way.

"Is that okay with you, Tilara?" March asked, looking at her.

"This Saturday? Day after tomorrow?"

"Well, maybe," he said, flashing his best smile. "Maybe next Saturday, but definitely a Saturday. You know, instead of a Friday."

She shrugged.

"Sure. Saturday...I mean a Saturday night sounds fine."

"March," Olivia said, "where's this big do gonna be?"

"Good question," said Braxton from Mr. Reese's rocker, where he'd sat after the old man had gone inside. "W-we should probably decide wh-wh-where before we pick the wh-when."

"Give the boy a gold star." Thumb did a flourish with his arms as he danced past Braxton on one foot.

"Thumb, you really do need to shut up!" Olivia's voice had an angry edge to it. It was a tone Thumb had never heard from Olivia, and it brought him to a halt.

"What's your problem?" he said, frowning.

"I don't have a problem," Olivia said, putting her left hand on her hip. "You the one making it impossible for us to get somewhere."

"Excuse me for breathing," Thumb said. He leaned against the building and pulled at his belt with his thumbs.

"N-not excused." Braxton chuckled. He sounded oddly like Mr. Reese.

"So, any ideas about where we should party?" The tone of March's question made it seem as if he already had the answer. "Actually, my house might be a good place."

"Yeah, March. You give great parties," Thumb said. He started snapping his fingers again, but his feet remained still.

"Sounds g-good to me," Braxton said, looking at Georgia out the corner of his eye.

"Fine with me," Olivia said. "How 'bout you, Tilara?"

"That sounds . . . I mean . . ." Tilara stopped herself and took a deep breath. Thoughts of the day at Morton's raced through her head. March had picked that place for the group to get together.

It's not okay with me. It will never be okay with me.

She looked down at her dress and picked at an invisible piece of string. "Sounds like you have a lot of parties at your house," she said.

March nodded, smiling. "Guilty," he said, sounding less humble than he might have hoped. "But I have to give my parents a lot of the credit. They love to entertain."

"That's great, but—" Tilara gathered her nerve as she spoke. "I mean . . . well, since you have parties at your house all the time, maybe it would be more fun for you to go somewhere else for our party."

"Maybe." March's satisfied smile dimmed. "Like where?" he asked.

"Like . . . well, like at my house," Tilara said, rushing her words. "I mean, it's really Aunt Cloelle's house. Where I'm living this summer."

"Miss Cloelle's house?" Olivia's voice and eyebrows rose at the same time.

"Yeah, why there, Tilara?" Thumb asked, giving March a sidelong glance. "Miss Haynes lives a long way from where the rest of us live."

"No, we . . . she doesn't," Tilara defended. "Aunt Cloelle lives halfway between here and there, I mean, between McKendree and Warren Springs, where you live."

Tilara struggled to fill the silence that followed. "Aunt Cloelle's yard would be a wonderful place for a party—an outdoor party."

Determined, she continued. "It'll be fun to have a outdoor party. I mean, the weather's great, and . . . we can do special things like string up lights, and . . . and it would be . . ."

Olivia jumped in, offering her support. "It would

202

be different. Real different! That's a good idea, Tilara," she said, grinning and then looking at March. "No offense, March, but I think we should do something different."

Pictures of himself and Tilara dancing under a dark sky and summer lights were already planted in March's mind. "Sounds perfect to me," he said. "Are you sure Miss Haynes won't mind?"

"I'm sure she won't," Tilara said. "Actually, Aunt Cloelle said something the other day about having a party for me before I leave to go back home."

Georgia got up from the steps where she had been sitting and listening. And frowning. "It won't be much of a party with just us," she said.

"Not much of a party? You got to be kiddin'!" Thumb started his dance again. "The MCs will be there. What more can anyone ask for?"

Tilara stood away from the support of the railing. "You could invite some of your friends from Warren Springs to come," she said.

Olivia's eyebrows and voice rose again. "You wouldn't mind having kids at the party you don't even know?"

"It's not just my party," Tilara said, resisting an urge to link arms with Olivia. "It's all of ours." She thought of Sylvie. And Sylvie's cousin Gloria, who had gone to the river with them one day. And Lucille.

She can bring her too-fine cousin.

Tilara grinned, finally caught up in the idea of having a party. "I know some kids who live near Aunt Cloelle, and I'd like to ask them to come, too."

Braxton got up from the rocker and walked over to Tilara. "It's nice of you t-to have the party," he said.

From where he had been standing, March needed to take only a step to move between Braxton and Tilara. He took it. "Very, *very* nice of you, Tilara," he said, smiling brightly. "Then it's settled. We'll have the party at Miss Haynes's. . . . Is next Saturday okay, Tilara?"

"Next Saturday's good. I mean . . . uh, I'll have to double-check with Aunt Cloelle, but I'm almost positive it'll be okay."

"We can make plans on Monday," March said, "like how many people and who's gonna bring what. You know, like food and pop and stuff." His voice deepened. "What we don't have to worry about is records for dancing. I got that covered."

"Parteeeee tiiiiiime!" Again Thumb twirled expertly, ending with a bow under the porch light. No one could resist applauding. Including Tilara.

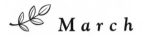 # March

March tilted his head back and stroked his neck with the liquid he had splashed into his hand. "Just a touch of sweetness," he said. "A little something in case I get kissin' close to someone tonight."

Thumb reached for the amber bottle and rubbed a few drops into his palms. "So, you goin' to put the move on Tilara tonight?"

March examined the shadow above his lip, hoping the fuzz had thickened. It hadn't. "If I can get past all that shy stuff."

"Maybe she's . . . already hung up on somebody," Thumb said. "Like somebody back where she lives."

March moved his hand across the hair he had brushed to smooth perfection. "Nah, that's not it. Tilara's shy. Haven't you noticed how she drops her eyes whenever you look at her?"

Thumb said nothing. March kept talking. "And how she kind of hangs back whenever we're just standing around— you know, like just talking."

"Yeah, maybe," Thumb said, moving to the mirror to take a closer look at himself. He reached for the ebony brush March had put down. "But Tilara's the one who got mostly everything going this summer. Like fixin' up the porch. That was her idea. And painting those old chairs we found in the basement—"

"That was Georgia's idea." March flicked pieces of lint from his sweater.

"Oh, yeah." Thumb smoothed back his hair as March had done. "But Tilara was the one who said I should paint that picture. And I don't think she even likes Miss Alpha all that much."

"So, who does?" March searched through the drawer where his father kept his handkerchiefs. "Look, man, I know what all Tilara did. I didn't say she wasn't smart. Just shy."

Thumb watched March tuck the spotless white square into one of his back pockets. "Maybe," he said, "but seems to me that she's not very shy around Braxton."

March had been examining his fingernails. His eyes narrowed as he looked over at the friend standing almost one-half foot shorter than he. "What are you talking about?" he asked in a tight voice.

206

"Nothin', man, nothin'." Thumb turned to look at himself in the mirror. "It's just that lately I've seen Tilara staring at Braxton," he said. "But she's probably just wondering why he's always makin' such a fool of himself over Georgia."

March added his image to the reflection, giving himself a final look of approval. "Yeah, Braxton really has a case for Georgia," he said, smoothing his hair again. "I ought to talk to her about that."

"And it's too bad he does," Thumb said, " 'cause I think Georgia has a case for you."

Satisfied that he was finally ready, March stood straight. He turned from the mirror and looked at Thumb. "Man, Georgia and me . . . we're like sister and brother. We been friends since before we started first grade. Good friends. That's what we are."

March threw his arm around Thumb's shoulders. "Com'on, man. It's time to get this party on the road!"

23

Tilara looked into the other face staring at her from the mirror. "Well?" she said, speaking to the reflection. "You going to keep staring or are you going to say something?" She glared at the other face and waited.

Finally, "Yeah, I'm gonna say something. You look so pretty, Tilara. Prettier than I ever seen you look."

Tilara turned away from the mirror, trying not to grin. Looking directly into Sylvie's face, she asked, "You're not just saying that, Sylvie? I really look okay?"

Sylvie's smile beamed. "You look a whole lot better than okay. Girl, you look good! I always been thinkin' you pretty, but now...How come you never wore that color before? It looks good on you."

Tilara wanted to cover her mouth and laugh out loud at the same time as a sudden shyness flooded through her. "Aunt Clo helped me pick it out. She said I should wear something festive."

Tilara turned to the mirror with the memory running in her mind. Cloelle asking her what she was going to wear to the party and the two of them going to the closet to pick something out.

"I have plenty of things I can wear, Aunt Clo," Tilara had insisted.

"Yes," Cloelle agreed, examining each garment she pushed back and forth across the closet pole. "But you don't have anything in a . . . a festive color."

Tilara looked at the line of soft-colored garments. Beige, cream, and pale greens and blues.

They're sensible colors, Tilara. Loud colors don't become you.

Hearing her father's words, Tilara turned up her nose. "I guess," she said, and shrugged. "But . . . they're okay." She reached for one of the dresses. "Like this one. This'll be fine for the party."

Cloelle took the hanger from Tilara and ran her fingers along the delicate bodice of the beige garment. "Hmm," she said. "It's lovely, baby. All your dresses are, but . . . well, I think they're a little too much on the . . . the quiet side."

Tilara took the dress from her aunt and hung it back in the closet. Her back was to Cloelle when she answered. "Uh, I don't look good in . . . in bright colors."

"Says who?" Cloelle challenged, placing her hand

on her hip. Then, as Tilara turned back around to answer, she held up the other hand to stop her niece. "Don't answer. I know exactly who."

A long moment passed as the two looked at each other. Then Cloelle said, "As I have pointed out on numerous occasions," she said, "my brother is a brilliant man and knows many things, including several wonderful stories." She put her arms on Tilara's shoulders. "But the story that tells how beautiful black skin should stay away from rich, bright colors is one sermon he ought *never* preach again!"

She looked deep into Tilara's eyes. "Think about it, baby," she said quietly. "Doesn't it follow that one beautiful shade put on this earth deserves to be next to another?"

Now, seeing herself in the full-length mirror and remembering her aunt's words, Tilara felt almost like saying amen. Instead she grinned and said to Sylvie, "And now that we're both festive, let's go outside and make sure the yard still looks as good as we do!"

Tilara and Sylvie stood together at the edge of the yard, looking at the results of the work they had finished that afternoon. The lanterns they had hung

shimmered above them, softly illuminating everything below. Dancing in the air under the lanterns
were red, green, white, and yellow balloons, each
anchored by a silver cord to one of the card-table
chairs they had set up in groups of four, five, and
six.

A line of lanterns marked a path to the big sugar
maple where the big-enough-for-two swing hung.
Tilara had found it in Cloelle's garage at the beginning of the summer, and Mr. Morris had put it up.
Its sturdy ropes were now wrapped with ribbons of
flowers, whose petals fluttered in the wind.

The for-summer baskets were filled with wildflowers from the meadow and hung along the porch
eaves wherever a space could be found. Along the
back of the porch they had set up the long table
Bessie had borrowed from the church kitchen, a
place for the food everyone was bringing. The table
was covered with a bright blue paper cloth. A bowl
of floating candles held down the cloth at one end,
and a vase of the fresh flowers Mick Morris had
brought anchored it at the other. Under the table
was a big tin washtub filled with ice and bottles of
pop. Across from the food table another small table
was set up to hold the record player and stack of
records.

Without a word the two girls turned to each other. Their smiles bloomed into satisfied grins.

"Girl, we are *gooooood*!" Sylvie said. Her words hung like music in the summer night air.

Tilara laughed without even a wonder about why she somehow was beginning to feel free.

Mick Morris came out onto the back porch from the kitchen, taking in every detail. Then he turned to Tilara and Sylvie. "It's beautiful, ladies," he said. "Beautiful."

"The balloons were Sylvie's idea," Tilara said, her eyes sparkling. "And the candles—" she gasped. "Sylvie, the candles! We forgot to light the candles in the yard."

Mr. Morris frowned. "Won't it be dangerous to have candles out here in the grass?"

"Bug candles," Cloelle said, coming out of the kitchen to join them. "Citronella candles to keep bugs away," she said.

She pulled matches from her pocket and handed them to Tilara. "Here, baby," she said. "You're lighting them in plenty of time."

She stroked Mick on his cheek. "And don't worry, my sweet," she said, "all the candles fit snugly in deep tin cans, and the cans rest in little grooves we dug in the ground. My two young ladies and I are nothing if not brilliant."

"Brilliance is a female trait," Tilara added, taking the matches and winking in Mick Morris's direction.

Watching Tilara and Sylvie go out into the yard, he called, "Ladies, are we ready to get this party on the road?"

"We certainly are!" Tilara called back.

"Then let's put on some partying music!"

He thumbed through the stack of records. After a moment, the sound of violins and the velvet voice of Nat King Cole drifted across the yard.

Looking at Cloelle, Mick Morris held out his arms. An invitation to dance.

"Hey, Mr. M.," Tilara called from the yard, "you volunteering to be our disc jockey tonight?"

"Sorry," Cloelle said, walking into the waiting arms, "but this deejay is off duty."

Mr. Morris shrugged his shoulders and called, "I tried," as he pulled Cloelle close.

Tilara and Sylvie looked self-consciously away from the two on the porch—and from each other, their faces set with determination not to giggle. And both with their own thoughts of what could lie ahead in the night.

Bending to light one of the candles, Tilara

glanced across her shoulder at the porch. Her aunt and Mick Morris had their arms around each other and were close together, dancing. Then she saw Mr. Morris lift Cloelle's chin to turn her face to his and bend slowly to kiss her.

Tilara looked away. Thoughts of being kissed tumbled around in her mind, and mixed with pictures of Braxton.

Kissing Braxton would be . . .

Her smile faded and her eyes dulled as she remembered. She gave herself a silent warning.

Forget it, Tilara. Just forget it.

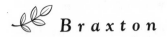 **B r a x t o n**

The car made a scrunching sound as it came to a stop. After Braxton and his father got out, Mr. Lewis walked slowly onto the lawn, enchanted by what he saw.

In the dusk the narrow band that stretched along the horizon glowed with the colors of a setting sun. It was as if two slender fingers had dipped into a pot of liquid roses and then moved gracefully across a gold-blue sky. Against these colors, the greens and red of McKendree were bold and brilliant.

"Your McKendree is beautiful, son." he said.

Braxton's walk was almost a run. "L-let's get to the building. I told Mr. Reese we'd be stopping by before the party. I hope he remembered."

"Where's the fire?"

The crackly voice came from the porch, where the slightly bent figure stood by the post next to the steps.

"Mr. Reese!" Braxton bounded up the steps, taking two at a time. "Wh-what are you d-doing out here?"

"What am I doing out here?" Mr. Reese leaned slightly on

215

the post. "You told me you'd be stoppin' by here this evenin', didn't you?" he said. "Where'd you expect me to be?"

As his father walked up the steps, Braxton dragged over the familiar rocker and placed it behind Mr. Reese. "Th-this is my father, Mr. Reese," he said. "Pops, this is—"

"Mr. Reese," Mr. Lewis said, coming up to the elderly man to shake his hand. "I've heard so much about you, feels like I already know you."

Extending the handshake, the older Lewis helped Mr. Reese resettle in the rocker while his son dragged over another chair.

"You got quite a boy here," Mr. Reese said, smiling and nodding. "It's been nice havin' him and the other young'uns around this summer. Real nice."

Braxton Lewis, Sr., nodded in agreement. "I think it's been good for all of them, too, although I don't think any of them thought they would enjoy themselves as much as they ended up doing." Mr. Lewis winked at his son, who had taken a seat on the steps.

"Aw, c-com'on, Pops," Braxton complained, but a smile was in his voice and eyes.

As the magnificent sunset faded, the night songs of the

frogs began. For a while the gentle creak of Mr. Reese's rocker was the only sound from the porch as the three sat silent and satisfied.

For Mr. Reese the visit was the satisfaction. His chance to look over the father of the boy he had grown to love over the summer, the young man he would have been proud to call his very own. His approval of the elder Lewis now helped him rest with contentment.

For Braxton Lewis, Sr., merely being asked to come and meet the much-talked-about Mr. Reese had brought great satisfaction. Proof that the bonding with his only child was going well. They had missed so much—all the years between Braxton's sixth and tenth birthdays. The years Braxton's mother had kept him after leaving the town she said smothered her. Now that he had Braxton back, any forging of that precious father-son bond was his every satisfaction.

For Braxton, stopping by McKendree was a special beginning to what he hoped would be a very special evening. A time to bring together two people he cared for deeply just before his time to let the girl of his thoughts know, finally, how he felt about her.

The two older men began reminiscing about days past

and good fishing along the New River. Around their tales Mr. Reese's cackle and Mr. Lewis's booming laugh came together, adding a new harmony to the night song that reached beyond the darkness.

24

Olivia was the first to bounce out of the car and onto the porch. "Hey, girl, this is nice!" she said. "It's pretty out here in the country."

Tilara laughed as she held open the door for Olivia and the others: Theodora and Joann, whom she had met that day at Morton's. And Georgia.

"Hi, everybody," Tilara said.

"I never knew it was like this down in the valley," Olivia said, her voice speeding as usual. "I only been over this way once or twice, you know, riding with my daddy. But he drives his taxi over this way a lot—that's him out there. He brought us."

"Olivia, slow down!" Georgia nudged Olivia on the arm. "We're gonna be here for a while." She looked over at Tilara, more from the corner of her eye than straight on. "Hi, Tilara," she said.

Tilara's welcoming smile was fixed on her face. "The party's out back," she said. "Com'on, follow me."

The four girls followed Tilara through the house, making their way carefully through Cloelle Haynes's softly lit living and dining rooms and kitchen. Three pairs of the eyes paid special attention to details of the warm, inviting home: the desert colors of the walls, the abundance of green, growing things, and especially the loud mews of protest coming from behind a closed bedroom door.

"It's Tut, our cat," Tilara said, chuckling at the questioning look on Joann's face. "He's probably mad because he wasn't invited to the party."

The remaining pair of eyes studied every detail of Tilara. The bright yellow of her dress against her dark skin. The matching yellow sandals. Her hair, usually a careless tangle, now carefully pulled back and swept up with small yellow flowers peeking through its twists and piles.

Leading the way, Tilara could feel the green-gray eyes on her. She made the doorway corner turns wider than she had to, crazily wondering for a moment if Georgia's dress billowed like her own.

It does match her eyes.

They were side by side when the group reached the porch. Tilara and Georgia, heading together out to the party.

"I'm here. Now the party can officially start!"

March made his announcement from the side of the yard where he and Thumb had entered.

"Hey, Thumb."

"March! Hey, man."

"We were wondering what had happened to you, March!"

March looked around. The timing was perfect. Most of the guests had arrived, but things were still a little quiet. Now that he was here, the party would get into high gear. He had no doubt about it.

He stood just outside the party parameter, the invisible lines marking its edges. It was an ideal spot for taking everything in—and for being seen.

From the top of his brown hair flecked with strands of dusty blond to the tips of his polished brown loafers, March was a handsome sight. Tall, lean, and brimming with confidence. His eyes twinkled, and his smile was broad.

"Hey, everybody," he called from his spotlight. "Sorry if we're late, but it takes time to make Thumb presentable."

Georgia walked over to March through the laughter that followed. "March," she said, "you never been on time for anything in your entire life." She stepped closer. "And I ought to know, 'cause that's how long we been knowing each other."

March caught Georgia around the waist. "So

what else you know about me, sweet thing?" he said in a voice louder than he had to.

"Ooooo, watch out! My man is talkin' stuff." Thumb began to do his dance.

Georgia shrugged away from March's teasing hug, but her cheeks flamed.

"Who's in charge of the music box?" March called out, gently spinning Georgia out and away so he could make his way over to the porch. "Whoever it is, I want you to know that help is on the way."

Within moments the tempo of the party changed. Where there had been muted voices, laughter rang out. Music that had been a quiet hum now invited dancing feet to the level places in the grass. Even the lanterns flickered brighter as they reflected the faces of the happy crowd.

Braxton came over to March, who had stopped by the food table. "Man, y-you really know h-how to get things going," he said.

"Nothing to it. Everybody's been ready," March said, grinning. "Me and the party just happened to get here at the same time."

Braxton dropped his eyes and shoved his hands into his pockets. It was a familiar stance when Braxton had something to say and one March knew well.

"So, man, what's goin' on? Who you pressin' tonight?" March asked.

Braxton looked into March's eyes. "March, i-is there any reason I shouldn't spend t-time with Georgia t-tonight?"

At first March looked back with a frown. Then, understanding, he broke into a wide grin. "Well, now," he said, patting Braxton on the back, "aren't you the gentleman." March laughed. "Man, for a minute there I didn't know what you were talkin' about."

He moved close to Braxton. "Georgia and I are friends," he said quietly. "Get it? Friends. We're like . . . like sister and brother." He patted Braxton again. "You know what I mean. It's like you and me—friends forever."

March leaned closer. "As far as I'm concerned," he said, "the only reason you *shouldn't* spend time with Georgia tonight is if you want her to spend time with Reggie, who's over there with her now, tryin' to make time."

Braxton followed the direction of March's eyes. He saw Georgia nodding as she listened to the very tall, well-built boy who had been the only freshman to make varsity squad of the basketball team.

March stepped back. "If I was you, I'd quit wasting my time talkin' to me. Good luck, my man," he said, giving Braxton a gentle shove.

"And now a clear field to Tilara."

The words sounded so good as he whispered them to himself, he wished he could shout them out loud.

March remained by the food table now weighed down with a magnificent array of sandwiches, ham, fried chicken, chips, brownies, cakes, cookies, stuffed celery, pickles, and salads. He looked over the spread, but his attention was not on eating.

"Tilara's inside," Olivia had said before returning to the yard with the plate she had filled up. "She went to answer the phone. She'll probably be right back."

He saw her the minute she pushed open the screen door. "Tilara!" he said.

"March." Tilara looked at him and smiled.

He walked over to her. "This is a terrific party. Almost perfect. Only one thing is missing."

"What?"

"You dancing with me."

March moved one step closer. As the melodies of "For Sentimental Reasons" filled the night, he held out his hand.

25

After the record ended, March held on to Tilara's hand and pulled her along with him, heading in the direction of the maple tree. A place far enough away from the music and laughter to talk— and be alone.

"March, wait," Tilara said, trying to slip from his grasp without jerking away her hand.

He stopped to look at her but did not let go of her hand. "Tilara," he said, "I want to talk to you. Just for a minute. I was thinking we could go where it won't be so noisy." He pointed to the swing. The crescent moon seemed to hang perfectly between its two garlanded sides.

"Okay, but I shouldn't stay away too long."

March continued on his way, gently holding on to the soft, cool hand.

Georgia watched March and Tilara until they disappeared around the corner of the house.

"Where are they going?" she whispered to herself.

She stood rooted by the trash box, where she had gone to dump her plate. While standing there, she had heard March and Tilara talking as they passed on the other side of the bush, but she hadn't been able to make out what they were saying.

She turned to head back to the center of the yard where everyone seemed to be gathered. Then, unable to make her feet go in a direction different from the one of her thoughts, she followed March and Tilara.

Georgia stopped near the climbing rosebushes and stood behind the white trellis that supported the trailing plants. Looking through the rectangles of the flower ladder, she kept her eyes on the two she had followed.

She watched as March put his arms around the bright yellow dress and pulled it toward him. Slowly. She could almost feel his hands as he placed them on the face above the dress. Tenderly. She caught her breath as she saw the smooth curve of his head bend to kiss the face he held in his hands.

It was more than she could bear.

Closing her eyes, Georgia jerked her head away from the rose-covered wall hiding her. The motion pushed her lip across one of the spiny green leaves, tearing her skin. She knew her lip was cut only when she saw blood on the hand she pulled back from her face. The hand she had put there to hold back her sad, angry tears.

"Tilara, what is it?" March took a short step back. He could feel her pulling away from his kiss. "Don't you know how much I like you? How long I've wanted to tell you?" His voice had never been softer or smoother.

March likes me?

"March . . . March." Tilara reached for the hand that was still on her face.

I don't believe this.

Realizing she was holding the hand she had removed from her face, she carefully let it drop. "March," she began again. "I . . . I mean, I don't know what to say."

"Say what you feel, Tilara. I am." March's smile had never been sweeter.

Aunt Clo was teasing me about March. I told her she didn't know what she was talking about. We almost had an argument about it.

A jumble of thoughts and words raced through

Tilara's head. They came together, making sense and nonsense.

"March . . ." Tilara pushed at her words. They seemed stuck in her mouth, on her tongue. "March, I really didn't—"

Is it stupid to say I really didn't know he liked me? And what if I had . . .

"Tilara, of course you know how I feel about you. We've been together all summer long." A smile danced in March's brown eyes. "You don't need to be shy now."

Lena will never believe this. Never. March likes me. Mr. Fine likes me. Me!

"March, I . . ." The words began to tumble out, almost as if they were pushing themselves. "I mean, I like you . . . as a person and everything, but not in . . . in the way you mean."

I never thought about kissing you. I never thought about you wanting to kiss me.

Tilara saw a strange look move across March's face. For a moment it made her want to reach out and touch him.

"And what *way* do I mean?" The smile on March's face seemed all at once frozen there.

Tilara looked away from the handsome face with the strangely frozen smile.

228

A way I have thought only about Braxton.

"A way that shows by . . . by being close and . . . and kissing," she said finally, looking into March's eyes.

"How do you know you don't like me that way?" March said through the smile that wouldn't change.

Because I never thought about you that way. Because I never thought you would think about me that way.

Tilara looked deep into March's face, testing the answer she wanted to give. "Because I just know," she said, now staring easily into the handsome, smiling face. "Because just about everyone knows who they want to kiss even before they do."

"And do you know who you want to kiss?" The smile was beginning to change just a little. Curving up and becoming a little ugly.

"Maybe. Sometimes." Tilara looked away.

Maybe not. Maybe I would have wanted to kiss you.

March moved back. Away from any touch of the billowing yellow dress that the wind brushed against his knees. "Then I guess all I should do is hope you get the kiss you want," he said. The frozen grin cracked and grew surprisingly wider.

March reached again for Tilara's hand almost the

229

same way he had done when leading her away from the grassy dance floor. But the hand Tilara felt holding her fingers was stiff. Still. Not inviting as it had been before.

"We'd better get back," March said. "I'm getting hungry. What about you?"

Braxton watched as March and Tilara returned, hand in hand. At almost the same moment, he saw Georgia going in the opposite direction. He took it as a signal. Time for him to act.

"G-Georgia," he called, catching up with her just before she turned the corner leading away from the party area. "You're n-not leaving, are you?"

Georgia whirled around, the sound of his voice surprising her. "Braxton," she said, staring as if to make certain the voice matched the face.

"Are y-you leaving?" he asked, coming closer.

"No," she said. "I was . . . I'm just going to get my sweater. I'm . . . ah, cold."

"D-d-do you mind if I come with you?"

Again Georgia stared, this time as if trying to understand what had been said to her.

"Yes. No . . . ah, sure. Come on," she said.

They began to walk together. Side by side.

"We s-stopped by McKendree on the way here."
Braxton's voice was light. Pleased. "Pops . . . ah, my
f-father, he met Mr. Reese. The three of us talked
t-t-together. It was nice."

Georgia said nothing. Braxton continued, "Mr.
Reese is r-really special. I'm glad w-w-we've gotten
to know him."

Finally, noticing Georgia's silence, Braxton
turned to look at her as they passed under a yellow
lantern. He saw the puffy scratch on her lip. "Your
lip," he said, stepping carefully in front of her.

His finger automatically reached out. It stopped,
suspended only a breath away from her face. "What
happened?" he asked.

"It's nothing," she said, moving her lips together
and patting them with her hand. "I . . . I bit my lip
chewing on some ice." She tried to laugh. "I'm
always doing something queer like that. Nana's
always telling me not to chew on ice. She says it
takes the enamel off your teeth."

"F-from the looks of things, it can also t-take the
skin off your lip."

Braxton was lost in the green-gray eyes that
looked up at him. Eyes too sad to belong even to the
downturned smile under them. He could not make
himself move away.

"If your n-nana were here, she would kiss your lip t-t-to make it better," Braxton said. "G-Georgia," he whispered, leaning close to her face to brush the corner of her lips with his own. It was the touch of a feather riding on the wind and landing in the grass.

Tilara stood under the blue lantern, the only blue one she and Sylvie had put up, even though there had been four in the box.

"These blue ones are the same color as the dress Mama and me bought for the party," Sylvie had said.

Then she lowered her lashes in that shy way she had. "Tee," she said, still looking down, "can we put up just one of these blue lanterns? That way it can be our special signal. Like if one of us needs help with something, gets nervous . . . or something else like that, the other will know just by looking under the lantern."

Tilara had known what Sylvie meant—and exactly how she felt. "That's a great idea, Sylvie," she had said.

After she and March came back, March had left Tilara under the blue lantern, telling her that he was going to get them something to drink. She was still standing there when Braxton and Georgia stopped under the yellow lantern directly across from the blue one. She stood frozen in the spot as Braxton bent down to tend Georgia's lip in his own special way.

When she felt the hand on her shoulder, Tilara just knew it would be Sylvie. Her newfound, wonderful friend. Not really knowing what particular "something" had come up, but coming to the blue lantern anyway.

But when Tilara turned around, it was Cloelle she saw.

"Sorry, baby," Cloelle said. "I didn't mean to frighten you."

Cloelle saw her niece's eyes. "You've heard," she said, her voice filled with caring.

"Heard what?"

"It looked like you were—" Cloelle put her arms around Tilara's shoulders. "Tee, I'm sorry to have to tell you this in the middle of the party, but you have to know. All of you do."

"Know what?"

"Mr. Reese has had a heart attack. A bad one."

Tilara stared at her aunt.

"Dr. P. has to leave right away, and we've got to make arrangements for the kids he drove here," Cloelle said.

Tilara found her voice. "Aunt Clo . . . ?" She held back the words she couldn't bear to hear herself say.

Cloelle rubbed Tilara's back. "Dr. P. feels . . . well, he thinks Mr. Reese probably isn't going to make it."

The tears Tilara had been fighting hard to hide fell in big drops from her eyes.

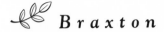 **B r a x t o n**

Braxton was the first one of them to get there. He came with his father, who said he wanted to go to the funeral, too. "Although I met Mr. Reese in person only that one time," the older Braxton Lewis said, "I've been getting to know him over the summer through you."

Now the two of them stood in the grass outside the small country church. Next to the narrow row of vehicles parked just beyond the trees: three cars and one hearse.

"I d-don't see March's dad's car or Dr. P.'s," Braxton said. "I guess n-none of the others are here yet."

Neither of them made any effort to move closer to the church or away from each other. They stood in the silence under the bright sun.

"Is Dr. P. bringing more than one carload from McKendree?" Mr. Lewis asked.

"I think s-so," Braxton answered. "He s-said he wouldn't be able to bring any of us. That's wh-why Olivia's dad is b-bringing everybody."

"What about the young lady that lives in the valley?"

Braxton looked at his father, not understanding at first. Then: "Oh, you mean T-Tilara."

A picture of Tilara flashed in his memory. Her running past him that night, her face streaming with tears. "She's c-coming with her aunt," he said, looking away from his father and toward the door of the church, an arch with darkness behind it. No break of light. No voices, no music.

"I w-wish there was music," he said. "Mr. Reese loved music." He swept the tip of his shoe softly across the top of the grass. "And the s-sound of the river. Mr. Reese loved being by that river. That's where w-we should be having s-something for him. Not here."

Braxton Lewis, Sr., laid his arm gently across his son's shoulders. "It doesn't have to be just here," he said.

As his shoulders warmed, Braxton looked into his father's face. "Yeah," he said. "W-we could have our own special s-service for Mr. Reese. At McKendree, by the river."

The sound of a car hummed in the distance. "I'll see what the others think wh-when they get here," Braxton said, looking toward the road.

Braxton Lewis, Sr., nodded. Then he tightened his hand on his son's arm to lead the way into the church.

26

Patting herself dry, Tilara stepped out of the tub and moved in front of the bathroom mirror. She studied the outline shrouded by the misty haze: a tangle of hair surrounding a head, a face underneath. Two long appendages pulling at a towel wrapped around the body.

It's like looking at myself through fog.

She turned to the small window behind her and lifted it open. The waiting breeze felt good on her face.

Turning back to the sink, she squeezed a ribbon of toothpaste onto her toothbrush and began to clean her teeth. The soft wind cleared a small, uneven spot on the mirror, revealing two fingers and a thumb holding the toothbrush and moving it up and down. The rest of the picture remained wrapped in the mist.

She bent over to rinse her mouth and then leaned farther into the sink to splash cold water on her face. Enjoying the coolness, she splashed it again. And again. She waited a moment to let the excess water drip away and then reached for the towel on the edge of the sink.

Raising the towel, she stood straight to pat her face dry. Then she opened her eyes. An image, now clear in every detail, stared back.

Tilara leaned closer, wondering at what she saw.

Rich brown skin without one blemish.

Like chocolate. A Hershey bar.

Full lips curving over even, glistening teeth. A long, proud neck.

She lifted her hand to pull back strands of hair caught in the dampness of her face. The fingers amazed her: graceful and slender with delicately curved nails.

She leaned closer to the mirror to look deeper into the wide, clear eyes with their nut-brown centers.

Haynes eyes.

Slowly, coming from deep within, a smile made its way across her face. She had no power—or will—to stop it as the familiar words rang in her thoughts. Aunt Cloelle's words. Ones so often stated, they had become a summer prayer: "Loving yourself is the very first step to anything, baby. Simply loving yourself."

⚘ M a r c h

Thumb stared at his friend stretched out on the lounge chair, wearing shorts and a T-shirt. "No way, man," he said, flopping down in the chair next to March. "Not even you can get away with that."

March took a sip from the bottle of pop he was holding. "What are you talkin' about, man? Get away with what?"

"With wearing what you have on to the . . . uh, what we havin' for Mr. Reese."

March put his head back and closed his eyes. "My clothes suit me fine for what I'm gonna be doin' this afternoon."

"You're not going to our . . . ah, to McKendree?"

March took another sip. "I went to the funeral, and that's plenty enough Mr. Reese services for me."

Just the mention of the funeral brought back the flower-sweet, awful smell that had been in the church. The smell that had brought back every memory of M'Dear so sharply, March was certain that if he looked, he would see her in that rectangle box for the dead at the end of the aisle. It would be M'Dear, resting against the cream pillows. M'Dear lying there just to prove that he would never again hear her voice or feel the love of her smile.

March leaned back in the long chair. "I've had enough services to last me a lifetime."

Thumb still sat at the edge of the chair. "So what are you gonna do?"

"Plan the party I'm gonna be havin' just before school starts." March closed his eyes. "McKendree has been a waste of time this whole summer. Now that our sentences are up, I ain't spending another minute there."

Thumb picked at the crease in his trousers. "But we all said we'd go?"

"Maybe the rest of y'all did," March said. "I didn't." He wiggled his bottle in the air. "Hey, man, you want some pop?"

"Naw. Thanks." Thumb took a deep breath and then asked, "Is it because of Tilara?"

March turned to him with narrowed eyes. "Is what because of Tee-lara?"

"Did you decide not to go today because of her?"

"What, because of her? What are you talkin' about?"

"I just thought maybe because you and her . . . well, you know."

March sat up and swung both legs around to one side of the bedlike chair. "You thought what? That maybe because Tilara and I aren't an item, I don't want to go to Mc-Kendree? Is that what you thought?"

March got up from the chair and pulled out one of the record albums from the shelf. "Thumb," he said, removing the black disc from its protective cover, "like I said, I'm not goin' today because I'm tired of being around folks that's old." He placed the record on the silver spindle of the player. "And like I said, I'm plannin' a party. A real party."

The sweet sound of Nat King Cole crept into the room.

"And as for Miss Tee-lara," March said, sitting back down, "there wasn't nothin' happening there. Anyhow, she'll be gone in a few days."

March reclined once more. "Man," he said, "did you notice Joann the other night at the party?"

"Joann?" Thumb started getting up.

"Yeah, Joann." March sank back further. "She's fine." He smiled. "And my party will be a perfect time to make sure she knows it."

March closed his eyes. "Perfect!"

27

Tilara brought together the final loops of the ribbon, completing the bow. Then she held the bouquet of flowers in front of her.

"It's lovely," Cloelle said from behind the screen door.

Tilara turned to look at her aunt. "Is it stupid to take flowers with me?" she said. "I mean, it's not a . . . a funeral, and there's no . . . you know . . ." Her voice faded as she turned away from the door and laid the bouquet carefully in her lap.

Cloelle came out and sat next to Tilara on the steps of the back porch. She began moving her hand up and down Tilara's back, rubbing it slowly.

"It's not stupid at all, baby," Cloelle said. "It's a lovely thing to do."

"I was thinking I might put it in Mr. Reese's rocker," Tilara said, "but that seems . . . you know, kind of maudlin. What do you think?"

Cloelle moved her hand from Tilara's back and rested it in her lap. "I'm sure Mr. Reese would consider it a wonderful gesture," she said after a moment.

The birds' afternoon calls bounced in the air. A joyous sound. A sound of life.

"I'll miss Mr. Reese," Cloelle said. "He was one of the heart reasons I looked forward to McKendree duty."

"Heart reasons?" Tilara looked at her aunt.

"One of the reasons making me feel good about being there," Cloelle said. "Some of the other reasons have to do with economics," she added.

"Everybody will miss Mr. Reese," Tilara said. "I will even when I'm back in Boston."

The two sat without speaking for a while, looking out at the everywhere mountains framing the outrageous garden.

"It's hard to believe our summer is almost over," Cloelle said, running her finger along Tilara's bare arm.

Tilara tilted her head against Cloelle's shoulder. "I don't *want* to believe it," she said, "and won't even try to until Papa gets here to whisk me away."

Both of them smiled, remembering Kenneth Haynes's proclamation the last time he had called from Boston. "You two have delayed Tilara's return to Boston twice," he boomed. "I'm coming down there to collect my daughter before you get a chance to do it again."

"It'll be good to see Kenneth here in the old home-place," Cloelle said.

"Yeah," Tilara said. It felt good to mean it.

Clouds passed over the sun, waving shadows over the greens of the mountains. The sun seemed brighter when the clouds moved on their way.

"Every time I start missing you terribly, I'm going to think about next summer, when you'll be back," Cloelle said, closing her eyes and offering up her face to the warmth of the sun.

"I'm going to insist that I leave the day after school is out!" Tilara's voice was strong.

Cloelle looked at her niece. "Insist?" she said.

"That's right," Tilara said with a determined nod. "And I'm going to start insisting when Papa gets here so he'll have plenty of time to get used to the idea."

"Good for you!" Cloelle playfully slapped her niece's knee. "And next summer we won't make McKendree such an all-consuming part of the agenda."

Tilara put her hand on her aunt's arm. "Aunt Cloelle, I didn't mind being at McKendree at all," she said. "It was . . . very special. I enjoyed it. Really." She caught Cloelle's hand in hers. "And I'd do it again next summer."

Cloelle grinned at her niece. "You would?"

"Yep," Tilara said. She lifted her face to the sun and closed her eyes. "I have heart reasons, too."

Saying no more, the two sat in the embrace of the mountains until it was time for the summer's last visit to McKendree.

28

Maggie Wilson stood on the long porch of McKendree, her back straighter than usual and the knot of hair on top of her head piled higher. Standing there next to Miss Alpha, who was hunched in her wheelchair, McKendree's head supervisor seemed more in command than ever.

The look of Maggie Wilson was as far from the truth of her as anything can be. Behind the dark eyes staring out at the group gathered on the slope was a flood of tears wanting to break through. Underneath that straight-as-a-rod back was a wish to curl up into a ball. A wish to give way to feelings filling her full as she listened to the singing coming from the river.

> "Oh, Glory,
> Oh, Glory.
> There is room enough in Paradise
> To have a home in Glory!"

The heart of Miss Wilson kept her still, straight, and strong. Especially strong. She had to be strong for Miss Alpha, for whom no day would ever again be quite as bright as those now gone.

Without turning her head, Miss Wilson looked at the old rocking chair, which now held a fragile bouquet of wildflowers. Then she looked down at Miss Alpha, whose wheelchair she stood behind.

Mr. Reese's "Brown Skin." The lips of the suddenly-old woman moved along silently with the words of the old spiritual both women knew well.

> "Oh, Glory,
> Oh, Glory,
> There's room enough in Paradise for me."

Braxton's strong tenor voice faded away as he put his guitar down on the ground beside him. After a long moment he got up. The others did the same.

Thumb bent close to Olivia's ear. "Olivia, did you hear that?" he whispered. "Braxton didn't stutter once while he was singing. Not once."

"Thumb, don't you start," Olivia hissed. "Not today."

"I'm not startin' nothing. Honest," Thumb said, keeping his voice low. "I just noticed that he sang without stuttering. That's all."

He reached for Olivia's hand and smiled. "But his singing was nice. Let's go tell him."

Thumb grinned at Olivia, enjoying the look of surprise on her face. It was the first time he had ever volunteered anything nice about Braxton. Or reached to take her hand. Every time before, it had been she who reached for his.

Georgia walked up to Tilara just as Olivia and Thumb walked over to Braxton. For the briefest moment the two girls faced each other without a word.

Tilara and Georgia. The two in the McKendree Crowd who had never gotten to know each other— or honestly tried to. Now they stood together under the late-morning sun. The momentary silence had no echoes of the fading summer.

Finally: "I bet you'll be glad to get back home." Georgia smiled as she spoke, pushing at her hair to keep it from blowing into her eyes.

Tilara smiled back. A new, easy smile. "In a way I will," she said, "but I'll miss being here. I'll miss it a lot."

Georgia raised her eyebrows. "You'll miss McKendree a lot?" Her laugh was almost a snort. "Not me. It might be strange not to be here, but it'll be a good strange."

Tilara chuckled. "I will miss McKendree, but mostly I'll miss being here in West Virginia," she said, "being with Aunt Clo."

"Yeah, Miss Cloelle is nice." Georgia pulled away the strands of hair clinging to her lips. "Will you be leaving soon?"

"This weekend." Tilara brushed at her cheek, feeling a speck of pollen. "My father is coming for a short visit, and we'll be going back to Boston together."

Georgia's smile broadened, and her eyes sparkled. "My mother's coming this weekend, too. She usually comes every summer and stays for a long time. At first it didn't look like she'd be coming at all this year, but finally she changed her mind."

Georgia's flow of words surprised her. She giggled in embarrassment, not noticing the warmth in Tilara's eyes.

"I know you'll be glad to see her," Tilara said, wanting to ask a question but deciding not to.

"Yeah. I will."

A second silence fell. One less comfortable than the first. Then: "Well, I'm gonna go up and say good-bye to Miss Alpha." Georgia's hands again fluttered toward her hair, this time not quite knowing what else to do. Later she would use them to reach out to the old lady on the porch. To give a hug. But not now.

Tilara looked into the green-gray eyes she had so often avoided and reached for Georgia's hand. "It was good to meet you, Georgia, and I hope you have a good visit with your mother."

Georgia felt the softness of Tilara's fingertips as she gently squeezed the hand in hers. "Thanks, Tilara," she said. "And I hope you have a safe trip home."

They smiled one last time together, each safely sealing her summer secret.

Tilara walked over to Braxton. He was putting his guitar back into its case. "Your song was . . . it was beautiful," she said.

"S-so was your poem, Tilara. Beautiful. Really b-b-beautiful." Braxton did not look up.

"I'm glad you decided to do this. It made me feel a little better." Seeing the outline of his jaw as she spoke, Tilara could tell that Braxton was clenching his teeth. "I also wanted to tell you how really sorry I am about Mr. Reese." She could feel herself clamping down on her own back teeth. "I mean, we all liked Mr. Reese so much, but it seemed like the two of you had something very special."

Braxton's head still hung over his guitar case. From where she stood above him, it seemed to Tilara that he was shaking his head.

"Braxton—" she started, but then stopped. There was nothing else she could say. Then, as she was about to walk away, Braxton got up.

The eyes that looked at Tilara brimmed with tears still to come. The face was wet with traces of those that had already fallen across his cheeks. "I loved him," Braxton said. "I r-really loved that old man."

Tilara moved closer to him. "And he loved you, Braxton. Everybody could see that," she said, stroking his hand.

Braxton nodded, then picked up his guitar case. He and Tilara headed away from the river and up the hill. Then, deep from the heart of a new inside picture, Tilara looked at Braxton and said, "I'd like to write to you. Would you answer my letters?"

"Sure," he said. His smile became a grin. "Why w-w-wouldn't I?"

"I just thought I'd make sure," Tilara said, continuing up the hill beside him.

"M-my letters always have a b-bonus," Braxton said, a laugh under his voice.

"What's that?"

"Every w-w-word comes out nice and s-s-straight!"

Tilara laughed and then bent over to take off her sandals. She wanted to enjoy the soft feel of the river grass between her toes one last time. She did not see Braxton's eyes grow warm and faraway. Eyes that followed the familiar yellow-brown curls falling next to Miss Alpha's head as Georgia leaned over to kiss the old lady good-bye.

29

Both of them had agreed on the plan: Cloelle
would go to the station to pick up Kenneth; Tilara
would wait for them at home. This would give Cloelle
some time with her brother—moments she could use
to help him realize that his lovely daughter was growing up. These moments would also give Cloelle a head
start in preparing Kenneth for next summer's plan.
First there would be a week or two in Boston and per-
haps even the Cape. Then Tilara would return with
Cloelle to spend the remaining months in West Virginia. There would be no argument about it. She and
Tilara had already made that decision as well.

Now, sitting on the edge of the porch with the
for-summer baskets and watching Tut bat at butterflies in the outrageous garden, Tilara smiled to herself at the thought of it all.

Papa, you're in for a bunch of surprises!

She pictured her father's face as he stepped off
the train. "Where's Tilara?" he would say right
away. "You mean, my daughter didn't even come to
the station to greet me?"

Hearing her father's voice in her mind, Tilara

mimicked one of his well-known scowls and then began to giggle.

"Oh, Kenny, you need to loosen up!" she said into the wind, loving the sound of it.

Leaning against the post, she looked up at the basket hanging directly above her head. It was her favorite, the one she and Cloelle discovered held just the right amount of fruit for a cobbler. It was the basket Cloelle's friend Nella had brought her from Jamaica, where she had grown up. That was another reason Tilara liked the basket more than the others. She and Cloelle dreamed out loud about being in Jamaica whenever they used it. Like the afternoon they picked up and carried the apples that had already fallen off the tree. Cloelle made them into applesauce. It was the first applesauce she had ever made, and it tasted terrible.

"Hey, mon, this is awful stuff," Tilara had teased, imitating Cloelle's friend. "I think we'd better get to the beach and feed it to the fishees."

That night had recorded another new picture. Like so many of the days and nights of their summer together. "I'm going to miss it here so much," Tilara said to the silent porch as she closed her eyes to burn all the pictures deep into her memory.

*　*　*

At the first sound of tires on the gravel, Tilara jumped from the porch into the yard and ran to the front of the house. She got there just as her father stepped out of the car.

"Papa!" She stopped at the edge of the walk with the word loud in her heart but quiet on her lips.

It was indeed her father. The Reverend Dr. Kenneth Cullen Haynes. Standing there beside Aunt Cloelle's car as tall and straight as he always was. And looking somewhat stern as he usually did.

But there was something else. . . .

Kenneth Haynes's eyes shone as he looked at his daughter. She seemed a little taller than she had in June, but that was to be expected. She was still a growing girl. And her hair was pinned up. He had never seen her wear it that way before. It looked . . . looked lovely that way. And she was wearing a bright green dress. He had never seen her in that color before. Strange choice, yet somehow it suited her. Yes, these were the differences. These were the changes. Changes to be expected.

But, still, there was something else. . . .

*　*　*

Tilara stared at this man she called Papa. Always. Even when Lena had teased and said it was a "baby word." But he *was* Papa. The man who used to carry her up to bed on his shoulders and who could make any book he read to her come alive.

"Papa's handsome. He's really handsome," Tilara whispered to herself, seeing the tall, imposing man before her in a new way. Getting an understanding of why her heart might have been won so completely by the tall, ebony-colored boy whose soft words often spilled out in small pieces.

She smiled.

As the wide smile graced his daughter's face, Kenneth Haynes grinned, too. It came as naturally as the sunrise.

"She's getting to be quite a young lady, our daughter," the handsome man whispered for only himself and the memory of his beautiful wife to hear.

Finally, the distance between them was closed. Kenneth Haynes wrapped his arms around his daughter and drew her close. "My Tilara," he said softly. "Just look at my Tilara!"

Tilara could feel the dampness on her father's cheek. Now safe within the circle of his arms, she squeezed him tighter and felt her heart smile.

*T*he sign at the fork in the road read MCKENDREE
12 MILES.

Each of the three passengers noticed the sign as the car
turned to take the other direction. The one marked PRINCE
C & O STATION. But they said nothing. They sat without
speaking as they had most of the way down the winding
mountain road.

When the car reached the train station, the silver-haired
driver got out and asked if they were going to wait for a while
in the car. All three nodded. The man remarked how good it
would be to see Esther again and headed to the station.

The girl among the three was the first to speak. Her curls
danced in the coming-fall winds blowing through the car's
opened windows. "What a strange coincidence," she said.

"Wh-what is?" asked one of the two boys.

"The name McKendree. It started our summer. In a way
it's ending it, too."

"McKendree ends everything," said the other boy. His
words were sarcastic and sharp, and his honey-gold eyes
flashed with anger.

The three grew quiet again, seeming content just to watch the scattered travelers on the platform. Then their eyes settled on the girl coming out of the small station house, and the three began to breathe almost as one.

She was a vision in red. A small red tam hugged one side of her head, framed by the cloud of sunflower-center brown hair. The cherry red suit was smooth in its newness. It hugged her, too, gently revealing certain facts of her standing-tall, becoming-woman's body.

Two others came out to join the girl. Standing there together, it was clear they were members of one family— one man, one woman, one girl in red.

Snatches of family loving drifted through the open car window.

"Kenneth . . . a wonderful summer . . ."

"Missed my daughter . . . the next time she comes . . ."

"Papa . . . Aunt Clo . . ."

Their words and laughter floated around them. The girl tossed her head back as she laughed. It was music.

There was a longing in the car to join the group and the laughter. But all three remained as they had been before— silent and still.

A train whistled in the distance. Soon it would pull beside the station on tracks running parallel to the river. The New River.

It was the end of a summer and of a time. Only memories would remain and be counted on to tell what had been.

McKendree.

AFTERWORD

There really was a place called McKendree. It nestled in a clearing along the banks of West Virginia's New River, which actually is the oldest river in North America. And in the 1940s McKendree really was an old folks' home for black people—Negroes, as many of us called ourselves then.

As a child I often visited McKendree with my father. It was usually on a Friday—the day of his weekly visit. On our way there my father would remind me of kindnesses I should extend. "Be sure to remember Miss Clark when we get there," he might say. "She always asks about you."

When I saw Miss Clark or Mr. Pate or Mrs. Jackson or whoever else my father had mentioned, I would talk a little and listen a lot. We would sit together on the long front porch facing the quiet river while the sun moved along the peaks of those glorious Appalachian Mountains.

The real McKendree disappeared long ago. In its place is a sprawling park. They named it "New River Park" after the river, which still flows from south to north. But McKendree has not been forgotten. Parts of it exist in the pages of this book. And, sadly, some of the ways we thought about ourselves in McKendree's time still creep into our attitudes today.

In addition to many memories of a wonderful father who took me to McKendree and was in some special ways the inimitable Dr. P., this book is lovingly dedicated to all who will one day come to know and believe in their own magnificent beauty.

—*Sandra Belton*

Sandra Belton at age 2 with her father.